WEDDING AT THE RIVERVIEW INN

MOLLY O'KEEFE

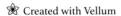

LETTER TO THE READER

Hi! Welcome to The Riverview Inn! A gorgeous lodge set in the Catskill Mountains, where we've got weddings, secrets, family and love. Lots of love.

A version of Wedding At The Riverview Inn was published as Baby Makes Three by Harlequin Superromance in 2007.

The rest of the series is:

Secrets of the Riverview Inn

Home to the Riverview Inn

Christmas at the Riverview Inn

Second Chance at the Riverview Inn

If you'd like more information about the rest of the series sign up for my newsletter.

Join my facebook group - The Keepers

Follow me on Bookbub!

I love hearing from readers so please feel free to drop me a line at molly@molly-okeefe.com.

My Book

DEDICATION

To Aunt Cherie and Uncle Earl
Sometimes, with family, you just get lucky.
And we are very lucky.

1

Out of the corner of his eye, Gabe Mitchell saw his father, Patrick, spit a mouthful of seaweed-wrapped tofu into his napkin like a five-year-old. Gabe kicked him under the table, appalled but envious.

"So?" Melissa, the chef responsible for the vegan spa cuisine, asked. "Was I right, or what?"

"Or what," Patrick muttered, balling his napkin up beside his plate.

"You were right," Gabe said and kept chewing. He chewed and chewed and the bland mouthful didn't break down. He was going to be chewing forever. "This is really something."

"Well?" She smiled broadly. "When do I start?"

Patrick laughed, but quickly coughed to cover it, so Gabe didn't bother kicking him again.

He managed to swallow the bite in his mouth, took a huge sip of the unsweetened berry smoothie to wash it down and was appalled to discover she'd somehow made berries taste bland, too.

He'd interviewed and auditioned five chefs and this one

really was the bottom of a very dark, very deep barrel. Not that he had any problem with raw food, or vegan food. It was the food with absolutely no flavor that was really disheartening. It was like she'd taken the flavor *out* of the food.

"Well—" he smiled and lied through his teeth "—I have a few more interviews this week, so I will have to get back to you."

The girl's eagerness turned on a dime and became narrow-eyed mean-spiritedness, which wasn't going to help her get the job. "You know," she said, "it's not going to be easy to find someone willing to live out here in the middle of nowhere."

"I understand that," he said graciously.

"And it's a brand-new inn." She shrugged. "It's not like you have the credentials to get a—"

"Well, then." He stood up and interrupted the defeating diatribe before she got to the part about how he was ugly and his father dressed him funny. "Why don't you gather your equipment and I'll call you if—"

"And that's another thing." Now she was really getting snotty. "Your kitchen is a disaster—"

That one hit him in the gut. Or maybe it was the seaweed finally working it's way through his system but he was suddenly at a loss for words.

"You know how building projects can be." Patrick stood, his silver hair and dashing smile gleaming in the sunlight. "One minute shambles, the next state of the art."

"You must be in the shambles part," Melissa said.

"Very true, but I can guarantee within the week state-of-the-art." His blue eyes twinkled as though he was letting Melissa in on a secret. It was times such as these that Gabe fully realized the compliment people gave him when they said he was a chip off the old block.

Patrick stepped to the side of Melissa and held out his arm toward the kitchen as though he were ushering her toward dinner, rather than away from a job interview she'd bombed.

Gabe sat with a smile. Dad was going to handle this one. *Great. Because I am out of niceties.*

"Tell me, Melissa, how did you get that tofu to stay together like that? In a tidy little bundle," Patrick asked as they walked toward the kitchen.

Melissa blushed and launched into a speech on the magic of toothpicks.

God save me from novice chefs.

The swinging door to the kitchen swung open, revealing his nowhere-near-completed kitchen, and then swung shut behind his father giving the terrible chef the heave-ho.

Gotta hand it to the guy, sixty-seven years old and he still has it.

Silence filled the room, from the cathedral ceiling to the fresh pine wood floors. The table and two chairs sat like an island in the middle of the vast, sun-splashed room.

He felt as though he was in the eye of the storm. If he left this room he'd be buffeted, torn apart by gale-force winds, deadlines, loose ends and a chefless kitchen.

"You're too nice," Patrick said, stepping back into the room.

"You told me to always be polite," Gabe said.

"Not when you are being poisoned."

Patrick lowered himself into the chair he'd vacated and crossed his arms over his flannel-covered barrel chest. "She was worse than the other five chefs you've talked to."

The seaweed-wrapped tofu on his plate seemed to mock Gabe, so he threw his napkin over it and pushed it away. At loose ends, he crossed his arms behind his head and stared out his wall of windows at his view of the Hudson River Valley.

The view was stunning. Gorgeous. Greens and grays and clouds like angels filling the slate-blue sky. He banked on that view to bring in the guests to his Riverview Inn, but he'd been hoping for a little more from the kitchen.

The Hudson River snaked its way through the corner of his property, and out the window, he could see the skeleton frame of the elaborate gazebo being built. The elaborate gazebo where, in two and a half months, there was going to be a very important wedding.

The mother of the bride had called out of the blue three days ago, needing an emergency site and had found him on the Web. And she'd been e-mailing every day to talk about the menu and he'd managed to put her off, telling her he needed guest numbers before he could put together a menu and a budget.

If they lost that wedding...well, he'd have to hope there was a manager's job open at McDonald's or that he could sell enough of his blood, or hair, or semen or whatever it took to get him out of the black hole of debt he'd be in.

All of the building was going according to plan. There had been a minor glitch with the plumber, however Max, his brother and begrudging but incredibly skilled general contractor, had sorted it out early and they were right back on track.

"Getting the chef was supposed to be the easy part, wasn't it?" Patrick asked. "I thought you had those hotshot friends of yours in New York City."

Gabe rolled his eyes at his father. Anyone who didn't

know the difference between a fuse box and a circuit breaker was a hotshot to him. And it wasn't a compliment.

"They decided to stay in New York City," he said. All three of his top choices, which had forced him into this hideous interview process.

Fifteen years in the restaurant business working his way up from waiter to bartender to sommelier. He had been the manager of the best restaurant in Albany for four years and finally owner of his own Zagat-rated bar and grill in Manhattan for the past five years and this is what he'd come to.

Flavorless food.

"I can't believe this is so hard," he muttered.

Patrick grinned.

"I open in a month and I've got no chef. No kitchen staff whatsoever."

Patrick chuckled.

"What the hell are you laughing at, Dad? I'm in serious trouble here."

"Your mother would say this—"

Icy anger exploded in his exhausted brain. "What is this recent fascination with Mom? She's been gone for years, I don't care what she'd say."

His cruel words echoed through the empty room. He rubbed his face, weary and ashamed of himself. "I'm sorry, Dad. I've got so much going on, I just don't want—"

"I understand, son." The heavy clap of his father's hand on his shoulder nearly had him crumbling into a heap. "But not everything can be charmed or finessed. Sometimes it takes work—"

"I work." Again, anger rose to the surface. "I work hard, Dad."

"Oh, son." Patrick's voice was rough. "I know you do. But

you've worked hard at making it all look easy. I've never seen a construction job go as smooth as this one has. You've got every lawyer, teamster and backhoe operator eating out of the palm of your hand."

"You think that's easy?" Gabe arched an eyebrow at his father.

"I know better than that. I've watched you work that gray in your hair and I've watched you work through the night for this place and I'm proud of you."

Oh, Jesus, he was going to cry in his seaweed. Though at least then it would be salty.

"But sometimes you have to make hard choices. Swallow your pride and beg and compromise and ask for favors. You have to fight, which is something you don't like to do."

That was true, he couldn't actually say he *fought* for things. Fighting implied arguments and standoffs and a possibility of losing.

Losing wasn't really his style.

He worked hard, he made the right contacts, he treated his friends well and his rivals better. He ensured things would go his way—which was a far cry from having them fall in his lap. But it was also a far cry from compromising or swallowing his pride or fighting.

The very idea gave Gabe the chills.

"You saying I should fight for Melissa?" He jerked his head at the door the vchef had left through.

"No." Patrick's bushy eyebrows lifted. "God, no. But I'm saying you should fight for the right chef."

"What're we fighting for?" Max, Gabe's older brother stomped into the room, brushing sawdust from the chest and arms of his navy fleece onto the floor. "Did I miss lunch?"

"Not really," Patrick said. "And we haven't actually started any fight, so cool your jets."

Max pulled one of the chairs from the stacks on tables in the corner, unclipped his tool belt and slung it over the back of the chair before sitting.

As the family expert on fighting, Max had made battles his life mission. And not just physically, though the bend in his nose attested to a few bar brawls and the scar on his neck from a bullet that got too close told the truth better than this new version of his brother, who, since being shot, acted as though he'd never relished a good confrontation.

Yep, Max knew how to fight, for all the good it did him.

"Well, from the look on Gabe's face, I guess we still don't have a chef," Max said, sliding his sunglasses into the neck of his shirt.

"No," Gabe growled. "We don't."

Now Max, his beloved brother, his best friend, stretched his arms over his head and laughed. "Never seen you have so much trouble, Gabe."

"I am so glad that my whole family is getting such pleasure out of this. Need I remind you that if this doesn't work, we're all homeless. You should show a little concern about what's going on."

"It's just a building," Max said.

Gabe couldn't agree less, but he kept his mouth shut. Going toe to toe with his brother, while satisfying on so many levels, wouldn't get him a chef.

"I'm going to go make us some lunch." Patrick stood and Max groaned. "Keep complaining and you can do it," he said over his shoulder and disappeared into the kitchen.

"Cheese sandwiches. Again," Max groused.

"It's better than what we had, trust me."

"What happened?"

"Ah, she fed us terrible food and then said I was crazy for trying to build an inn in the middle of nowhere and get a chef to come out here for little pay in a half-finished kitchen. Basically, what all the chefs have said to me."

Gabe paused, then gathered the courage to ask the question that had been keeping him up nights.

"Do you think they're right? Is it nuts to expect a high-caliber chef to come way out here and put their career on the line and their life on hold to see if this place takes off?"

Max tipped his head back and howled, the sound reverberating through the room, echoing off the vaulted ceiling. "Brother, I've been telling you this was nuts for over a year. Don't tell me you're starting to agree now!"

Gabe smiled. He was discouraged, sure. Tired as all hell, without a doubt. Frustrated and getting close to psychotic about his chefless state, absolutely. But his Riverview Inn was going to be a success.

He'd work himself into the hospital, into his grave to make sure of it.

He had been dreaming of this inn for ten years.

"It's not like I've got no credentials." He scowled, hating that Melissa had gotten under his skin and that he still felt the need to justify his dream. "I worked my way up to manager in the restaurant in Albany. And I owned one of the top ten restaurants in New York City for five years. I've had reporters and writers calling me for months wanting to do interviews. The restaurant reviewer for *Bon Appetit* wanted to come out and see the property before we even got started."

"All the more reason to get yourself a great chef."

"Who?" He rubbed his hands over his face.

"Call Alice," Max said matter-of-factly, as though Alice was on speed dial or something.

Gabe's heart chugged and sputtered.

He couldn't breathe for a minute. It'd been so long since someone had said her name out loud. *Alice.*

"Who?" he asked through a dry throat. Gabe knew, of course. How many Alices could one guy know? But, surely his brother, his best friend, had not pulled *Alice* from the past and suggested she was the solution to his problems.

"Don't be stupid." Max slapped him on the back. "The whole idea of this place started with her—"

"No, it didn't." Gabe felt compelled to resist the whole suggestion. *Alice* had never, ever been the solution to a problem. She was the genesis of trouble, the spring from which any disaster in his life emerged.

Max shook his head and Gabe noticed the silver in his brother's temples had spread to pepper his whole head and sprouted in his dark beard. This place was aging them both. "We open in a month and you want to act like a five-year-old?" Max asked.

"No, of course not. But my ex-wife isn't going to help things here."

"She's an amazing chef." Max licked his lips. "I can't tell you the number of times I've woken up in a cold sweat thinking of that duck thing she made with the cherries."

Gabe worried at the cut along his thumb with his other thumb and tried not to remember all the times in the past five years he'd woken in a cold sweat thinking of Alice.

"Gabe." Max laid a hand on Gabe's shoulder. "Be smart."

"Last I heard she was a superstar," Gabe said. He tried to relax the muscles of his back, his arms that had gone tight at the mention of Alice. He tried to calm his heart. "She wouldn't be interested."

"When was the last you heard?"

It's not as though she'd stayed in touch after that first

year when they'd divvied up all the things they'd gathered and collected—the antiques from upstate, their kitchen, their friends. "About four years ago."

"Well, maybe she'll know of someone. She can at least point you in the right direction."

Gabe groaned. "I hate it when you're right," he muttered.

"Well, I'd think you'd be used to it by now." Max laughed. "I think I'll skip lunch and get back to work." He grabbed his tool belt. "The gazebo should be done by tomorrow."

"What's the status on the cottages?" Gabe asked.

"You'll have to ask Dad." Max shrugged his broad shoulders and cinched the tool belt around his waist, over his faded and torn jeans. "As far as I know he just had some roofing and a little electrical to finish on the last one."

Gabe's affection and gratitude toward his brother and dad caught him right in the throat. The Riverview Inn with its cottages, stone-and-beam lodge and gazebo and walking trails and gardens had been his dream, the goal of his entire working life. But he never, ever would have been able to accomplish it without his family.

"Max, I know I don't say it enough, but thank you. I—"

Max predictably held up a hand. "You can thank me by providing me with some decent chow. It's not too much to ask."

He took his sunglasses from the neck of his fleece and slid them on, looking dangerous, like the cop he'd been and not at all like the brother Gabe knew.

"Oh, I almost forgot," Max said, poised to leave. "Sheriff Ginley has got two more kids."

"Can either of them cook?"

Max shrugged. "I think one of them got fired from McDonald's."

"Great, he can be our chef."

"I don't think Sheriff Ginley would smile upon a juvenile delinquent with such easy access to knives."

The after-school work program for kids who got in trouble in Athens, the small town north of the inn, had been Max's idea, but Gabe had to admit, the labor was handy, and he hoped they were doing some good for the kids. "They can help you with the grounds."

"That's what I figured." Max smiled wickedly and left, his heavy-booted footsteps thudding through the nearly empty room.

Gabe sighed and let his head fall back. He stared up at the elaborate cedar joists in the ceiling, imagined them with the delicate white Christmas lights he planned on winding around them.

The ceiling would look like the night sky dotted with stars.

It had been one of Alice's ideas.

He and Alice used to talk about opening a place out of the city. A place on a bluff. He'd talked about cottages and fireplaces and she'd talked about organic ingredients and local produce. They'd been a team then, she the chef, he the consummate host, producer and manager. He'd felt invincible in those early days with Alice by his side.

But then the problems came and Alice got more and more distant, more and more sad with every trip to the doctor, every failed effort that ended in blood and tears and —Well, he'd never felt so helpless in his life.

"Lunch, boys!" Dad called from the kitchen the way he had since their mom walked out on them more than thirty years ago.

Gabe smiled and stood.

Nothing to do but eat a cheese sandwich and get to work. His dream wasn't going to build itself.

The hangover pounded behind Alice's eyes. Her fingers shook, so she set down the knife before she diced up her finger along with the tomatoes.

"I'm taking a break," she told Trudy, who worked across from her at the long stainless steel prep table.

Trudy's black eyes were concerned. "That's your second break since you've been here and it's only three."

"Smoker's rights," Alice croaked and grabbed a mug from the drying rack by the industrial washer and filled it with the swill Johnny O's called coffee.

"You don't smoke," Trudy pointed out, trying to be helpful and failing miserably. "If Darnell comes back here, what am I supposed to tell him?"

"That he can fire me." Alice slid her sunglasses from her coat hanging by the door and used her hips to push out into the bright afternoon.

Even with her dark glasses on, the sunshine felt like razor wire against her eyeballs, so after she collapsed onto the bench that had been set up by the dumpsters for staff, she just shut her eyes against the sun.

The hangover, the sleeplessness, this mindless menial job that paid her part of the mortgage, it all weighed her down like sandbags attached to her neck.

Tonight no drinking, she swore.

She couldn't change the fact that she'd fallen from chef and owner of Zinnia's to head line chef at one of the three

Johnny O's franchises in Albany. That damage was already done and she'd come to grips with it.

But she could control the drinking.

A small voice reminded her that she made that promise almost every night.

Sometimes she wanted to punch the small voice, but instead she breathed deep of the slightly putrid air and tried to get Zen about the whole situation. She took a sip of her coffee, and listened to the sound of traffic.

The parking lot was pretty empty, but soon the hungry folks of Albany would be getting off work and looking for a sunny patio and drink specials and a lot of them would head to Johnny O's. The kitchen would be loud and on fire for about eight hours and in those eight hours, while arranging plates of pasta and fire-baked pizzas and grilling steaks and fish specials, she would forget all the reasons she had to drink.

Maybe she'd help the cleaning staff tonight. Work herself into a good exhaustion so she wouldn't need the red wine to relax.

She tilted her face up to the sun and stretched out her feet, pleased with her plan.

A black truck, mud splattered and beat-up, pulled in to the lot and parked directly across from her. She thought about heading back inside, or at least opening the door and yelling to warn Trudy customers were arriving and the kitchen was on demand. But Trudy had been in the business as long as she had and could handle cooking for a truckload of guys.

But only one guy got out.

One guy, holding a droopy bouquet of yellow roses.

One guy, whose slow amble toward her was painfully, heartbreakingly familiar.

Coffee sloshed onto her pants, so she set the cup down on the bench and clenched her suddenly shaking hands together.

Spots swam in front of her eyes and her head felt light and full, like a balloon about to pop.

The man was tall and lean, so handsome still it made her heart hurt.

He stopped right in front of her and pushed his sunglasses up onto his head, displacing his dark blond hair. The sun was behind him and he seemed so big. She used to love his size, love how it made her feel small and safe. He'd wrap those strong arms around her and she felt protected from the world, from herself.

He smiled like a man who knew all the tastiest things about her.

That smile was his trademark. He could disarm an angry patron at four feet with the strength of his charming smile. He could woo frigid reviewers, disgruntled suppliers...his ex-wife.

"Hello, Alice." He held out the roses but she couldn't get her hands to lift and take them.

She left her shades on, so shattered by Gabe's sudden appearance in front of her, as if the past five years hadn't happened.

"Gabe." Her voice croaked again and she nearly cringed.

He took a deep breath, in through his nose, no doubt hoping for a bit more welcome from her, some reaction other than the stoic front that was all she had these days.

His hand holding the roses fell back to his side.

"What are you doing here?" she asked. She sounded accusatory and mean, like a stranger who had never known him at all.

And she felt that way. It was why, in part, the marriage

had ended. Despite the late-night talks, the dreams of building a business together, the sex that held them together longer than they should have been, in the end, when things got bad, they really never knew each other at all.

"I could ask you the same thing." His eyes swept the bench, the back door to Johnny O's. The Dumpsters.

Suddenly, the reality of her life hammered home like a nail in her coffin. She worked shifts at a chain restaurant and was hungover at three on a Friday afternoon.

Oh, how the mighty have fallen, she thought bitterly, hating herself with a vehemence she usually saved for her dark drunken hours.

"I work here," she said, battling her embarrassment with the sharp tilt of her head.

He nodded and watched her, his blue eyes cataloging the differences the five years between them had made. And behind her sunglasses, she did the same.

Gabe Mitchell was still devilishly easy on the eyes.

He'd always had her number. One sideways look from him, one tiny grin and she'd trip over her hormones to get into his arms. There was just something about the man and, she surmised after taking in his faded jeans and the black T-shirt with the rip at the collar, the work boots and his general all-around sexiness, there still was something about him.

But, she reminded herself, underneath that lovely candy coating beat one cold, cold heart. She'd learned it the hard way, and she still hadn't recovered from the frost burn her five-year marriage had given her.

Call it fear of commitment, call it intimacy issues, whatever it was, Gabe had it bad. And watching him walk away from her and their marriage had nearly killed her.

"You look good," Gabe said and it was such a lie, such an attempt to sweet-talk her, that she laughed. "You do," he protested.

"Save the charm for someone else, Gabe." Finally she pushed her shades up onto her head and looked her ex-husband in the eye. "I told you I never wanted to see you again."

2

"And—" his smile seemed a little brittle around the edges "—I think we both know you didn't mean it."

She arched her eyebrows in response. Oh, she'd meant it all right.

"What do you want, Gabe?"

"A guy can't visit an old friend?"

She laughed outright. At him. At them. At this stupid little dance.

"Gabe, we were never friends." The lie slipped off her tongue easily. It was better to pretend they had never been friends than to dwell on those memories, to give in to the sudden swell of feelings his presence stirred in her belly. "What. Do. You. Want?"

He ran his fingers through his too-long hair and scowled at her, the fierce look that always warned her he was running out of patience.

Good, she thought, *get mad and leave like you always do.*

She scowled back. She'd never been overly gracious—

she was too busy for that—but in her time with Gabe she'd learned to be polite.

But not anymore. There was no one in her life to be polite to, so she had no practice.

And she wasn't about to apologize. Not to him.

"I need you," he said and she fought to keep herself from choking on a sound of disbelief.

"Gabe Mitchell at my door, begging." She shivered dramatically. "Hell is getting colder."

"Alice." He sighed. "This isn't easy for me. You know that. But I need you. Bad."

His low tone hit her in the stomach and snaked down to her sex, which bloomed in sudden heat. Too familiar, those words. Too reminiscent of those nights together, when they'd needed each other so much, good sense got burned to ash.

"I really can't imagine why," she said, crossing one leg over another, and her arms came across her chest, giving him every signal to stop, to say goodbye and walk away.

But he didn't and she wondered what was truly at stake here. The Gabe she knew did not fight and he never begged.

"I built the inn," he said softly. "The one we always talked about."

It was a slap. A punch in her gut. Her eyes burned from the pain and shock of it. How dare he? He'd walked away with her pride, her self-respect, her dreams of a family and now this.

She wanted to scream, just tilt her head back and howl at the pain and injustice of it all.

The inn. The home they'd dreamed of. He'd built it while she worked shifts grilling grade B steak and making nachos.

19

She let out a slow breath, emptying her body of air, so maybe the shell she was would just blow away on the wind.

"Good for you," she managed to say through frozen lips and got to her feet. "I need to go."

He stopped her, not by touching her—good God wouldn't that be a disaster—but by getting in her way with his oversize body.

"It's gorgeous, Alice, you should see it. I named it the Riverview Inn and it's right on a bluff with the Hudson snaking through the property. You can see the river from the dining room."

A mean anger seeped into her, culled from her crappy job, her hangover, her ruined life...even from the Dumpster. She didn't need to be reminded of how much she'd lost and she really didn't need to be brought face-to-face with how well Gabe had done.

"Like I said—" she didn't spare the sarcasm "—bully for you. I'll tell all my friends." She ducked by him.

"I need a chef, Alice."

She stopped midstride, snagged for a second on a splinter of hope. Of joy.

Then she jerked herself free and laughed, but refused to meet his earnest blue eyes. Was this real? Was this some kind of trick? A lie? Were the few remaining friends in her life setting up some elaborate intervention?

"Me? Oh, man, you must be in some dire straits if you are coming to me—"

"I am. I am desperate. And—" he inclined his head to the Dumpster, the plaza parking lot "—from the look of things...so are you."

The bravado and sunglasses didn't work. He saw right through her and it fueled her bitter anger.

"I'm fine," she said, stubbornly clinging to her illusions. "I need to get back to work."

"I want to talk to you about this, Alice. It's a win-win for both of us."

"Ah, Gabe Mitchell of the silver tongue. Everything is a win-win until it all goes to shit. No." She shook her head, suddenly desperate to get away from him and his magnetic force that always spun her in circles. "I won't be your chef."

She walked around him, careful not to get too close, not to touch him, or smell him, or feel the heat from his arm.

"I know where you live, Alice," he said, going for a joke, trying to be charming. "Look, I just want to talk. If you decide after we talk that it's not for you, fine. That's totally fine. But maybe you know someone—"

"I don't."

"Alice." He sighed that sigh that weighed on her, that, during their marriage, had filled the distance between them and pushed them further apart. The sigh that said, "Don't be difficult."

"I don't," she insisted. "I don't know anyone who would want to live out there."

"Except you?" Gabe said.

"Not anymore," she lied. "My break is over. I have to go."

"I want to talk. Can I meet you at home?" He caught himself. "At your house?"

Painful sympathy leaped in her. He'd loved their house, had craved a home, some place solid to retreat to at the end of the day. He'd finished the basement and hung pictures and shelves and repaired the bad plumbing like a man in love. And in the divorce he'd given it to her, shoved the lovely Tudor away like a friend who'd betrayed him.

"The locks are changed," she said.

"I'm sure they are, but I'll bet you a drive out to the inn

that you still keep the key under that ceramic frog you bought in Mexico." He smiled, that crooked half grin. Charm and bonhomie oozing off him and she wanted to tell him no matter how well he thought he knew her, he didn't.

But the key *was* under the frog.

"Suit yourself, Gabe," she told him. "But my answer won't change."

"Alice—"

He held out the roses and she ignored them. She hit the door and didn't look back. She could feel him, the touch of his gaze even through the steel door, through her clothes, through her skin right to the heart of her.

Nope, she shook her head. Not again. Not ever again with that man. She'd worked too hard to forget the past. She'd worked too hard to stop the pain, to cauterize the wounds he'd left in her.

There was nothing he could say that would convince her. Nothing.

∾

"Well," Gabe said, tossing the bouquet into the Dumpster. "That went well."

He shook off the strange sensation in his stomach, brought on by the begging he'd had to do just to get her to listen to him.

Dad would be proud, he thought and the thought actually made him feel better.

He still couldn't manage to wrap his head around the fact that she worked at Johnny O's. Last he'd heard, her restaurant, Zinnia or Begonia or something, had gotten a high Zagat rating and someone had approached her about doing a cookbook.

He looked at the neon lights of the cookie-cutter restaurant she'd escaped into and smiled.

This had to bode well for him. She must be dying to get out of this place. He just had to figure out what kind of offer would make her see things his way.

First things first, he'd stop by the house, take stock of her kitchen, run for groceries and have some food waiting for her. Tomato soup and grilled-cheese on sourdough bread, her favorite. Followed up by mint Oreos—another favorite. Maybe he'd get the Beaujolais she loved, set up some candles...

A seduction. He smiled thinking about it, even when something primitive leaped in his gut. It was weird, but he'd set up a sexless chef seduction of his ex-wife.

Whatever it took.

He headed to his truck, climbed in and on autopilot wound his way through Albany to the lower east side. By rote he turned left on Mulberry, right on Pape and pulled in to the driveway of 312.

He took a deep breath, bracing himself.

Empty houses with dark windows disturbed him, ruffled those memories of being a boy and wondering if, when he went downstairs, she would finally be there. If this morning, after all the others, would be the one when the kitchen would be warm, the lights on, the smell of coffee and bacon in the air, and Mom would be sitting at the table. She'd tell him it all had been a mistake and she wouldn't be leaving, ever again.

Stupid, he told himself. *Ancient history. Like my marriage. It's just a house. It's not mine anymore.*

Finally he looked up at the two-story Tudor—with its

big backyard—where they'd planned to start their family. The magnolia tree out front was in full bloom, carpeting the lawn in thick creamy pink and white petals.

Her herb garden looked a little overrun with chives and she must have finally decided that perennials weren't worth the hassle. Otherwise the house looked amazing.

Sunlight glittered off the leaded windows and he tried not to remember how he'd jumped on the house, probably paying too much. But it hadn't mattered at the time—the house was meant to be theirs.

And it had been a happy home for a year.

His neck went hot and his fingers tingled. He forced himself to fold the feelings up and shove them back in the box from which they'd sprung.

Don't care, he told himself ruthlessly, hardening his heart. He let himself go cold, pushing those memories away with the ones of his mother until his heart rate returned to normal, his fingers stopped tingling.

It's just a building. Not my home.

He got out of the truck and bounded up the slate walkway.

He lifted the blue frog with the bulging eyes that sat on her porch and—as expected—there was the key. But he couldn't pick it up. His body didn't obey the messages from his brain. His body wanted to run.

"Hey, man? You need something?" Gabe whirled to find a good-looking, tall...kid. Really. Couldn't have been older than twenty-six. He stood in the open doorway, a backpack slung over his shoulder.

"Hi," Gabe started to say. "No. Well, yes. Actually."

"You selling something?" The kid pointed to the sign Alice had hand printed and posted on the mailbox: No

Salesmen, No Flyers, No Religious Fanatics. This
Means You.

He smiled, typical Alice.

"No," he told the kid. "I'm not selling anything. My name
is Gabe and I—"

"You're the dude in the pictures." The guy smiled and
held out his hand. "You look good, keeping in shape."

Gabe was knocked off stride but managed to shake his
hand anyway. "Thanks. Um... I'm sorry, who are you?" *And
what pictures?*

"Charlie, I'm Alice's roommate."

Roommate? Gabe's mouth fell open.

"No, no, man, not like that." The kid laughed. "Though I
did try at the beginning but she pretty much let me know
that wasn't going to be happening. I just pay rent and live in
the basement."

"Why does she need a roommate?" he asked.

Charlie shrugged. "Why does anyone need a roommate? Money, I guess. It's not for the company that's for
sure. I barely see her anymore. She used to make me
dinner." He whistled through his teeth. "Best food I ever
had."

Gabe's head reeled, but he saw the sugar he needed to
sweeten the deal. Alice needed money, it was the only way
his incredibly private ex-wife would ever rent out part of her
home and, horrors, share her kitchen with some kid who no
doubt scarfed down freeze-dried noodles and Lucky
Charms by the boatload.

Perhaps it wouldn't be so hard to convince her—working
at Johnny O's, renting out the basement. He only needed to
push down her pride and get her to see what an opportunity
he had for her.

"She *is* a great chef," Gabe said. "Look, Charlie. If you

don't mind, I was hoping to come in and wait for Alice to get home. I am supposed to have a business meeting with her."

"Sure, no problem." Charlie stepped out onto the porch, leaving the heavy wooden storm door open. "Don't touch her booze, though. She gets crazy if you drink her stuff."

Gabe nodded, suddenly speechless as Charlie walked by dragging with him Alice's scent from the house. Roses and lemon swirled out around him, reminding him of the smell of her blue-black curls spread out across the pillows of their marriage bed, the damp nape of her neck after a shower.

"See you around," Charlie said and took off on a bike.

Gabe lifted his hand in a halfhearted farewell.

Suddenly, the narrow hallway leading back to the living room with its big picture windows looked a mile long.

The brass key in his hand—a standard house key, identical to the one he'd carried on his key chain for years—weighed a thousand pounds.

Need a chef. Need a chef. Need a chef.

He wished it didn't require going into that house.

He took a deep breath, buffered himself against the ghosts inside and stormed the gates. Immediately he was caught short by the familiarity of their home.

The foyer still had the cut-glass vase filled with overblown pink roses in it—she'd always loved putting it there—and the walls were adorned with their photos. Black-and-white shots from their various trips. Those were the pictures Charlie had referred to. Gabe was in some of them, standing next to the Vietnamese fisherman and the Mexican grandmother who made the best tortillas he'd ever tasted.

What is she doing with these still on the wall? He wondered. He'd emptied all his frames of her, his wallet and photo albums. Looking at his apartment, you'd never guess he'd been married. Looking at her house, you'd never guess she'd been divorced.

He stalked through the house and turned right toward the kitchen, resisting the urge to check out the family room and the back lawn.

More roses sat on the kitchen table. These were fresh, bright yellow buds still.

The kitchen was spotless. Their expensive renovation still looked modern and elegant, such a reflection of his wife.

Ex-wife. Ex.

An image—one of the few to have survived the war between him and Alice—came and went like smoke in sunshine.

The memory was of a random night—a Wednesday or something in March—when nothing special was happening. Alice had come home late from shutting down the restaurant and he'd woken up while she showered. He'd waited for her in this kitchen, dark but for the bright panels of moonlight that lay over the furniture like a sheet. She'd walked in wearing a pair of boxer shorts and nothing else.

She'd smelled sweet and clean. Powdery. Her hair a dark slick down her back. Her lithe body taut and graceful, her skin rosy and fresh.

"You're better than sleep," she'd said to him, pressing a kiss to the side of his neck, just south of his ear. He'd touched her back, found those dimples at the base of her spine that he'd loved with dizzying devotion.

And then they'd made slow, sleepy lazy love.

It surprised him at odd times when it seemed as though his Alice years had happened to someone else. When he thought he'd finally managed to put it all behind him.

But looking at his former kitchen, the memory

ambushed him, rocked him on his heels and had him struggling for breath that didn't taste of his ex-wife.

He tore open the maple cabinets, as if he could tear that stubborn memory out of his brain. But in cabinet after cabinet he only found empty shelves. Which was not at all like her. She used to say that having an empty pantry made her nervous. If there wasn't pasta, garlic and olive oil on hand at all times she wouldn't be able to sleep at night.

Something in his gut twinged. Remorse? Worry?

No, couldn't be. He was divorced. Papers, signed by both of them, exonerated him from worry and remorse.

But his gut still twinged.

He pulled open the cabinet above the fridge only to find it fully stocked with high-end liquor.

No need for the Beaujolais.

Another cabinet over the chopping block was filled with freeze-dried noodles and cereal.

Charlie's small stake in the kitchen.

Something warm and fluffy brushed up against his ankles and he looked down to find Felix, their French cat. Another thing she'd gotten in the divorce.

"*Bonjour*, Felix," he said with great affection. The gray-and-white cat wasn't really French—he was south-side Albany Dumpster—but they considered him so due to his love of anchovies, olives and lemon juice.

Gabe opened the fridge and found enough anchovies and expensive olives soaked in lemon juice to keep the cat happy for eons.

He pulled out a slick, silver fish and fed it to the purring cat. "What's happening here, Felix?" he asked, stroking the cat's ears.

During their last big fight, Alice had told him that she would be better off without him. Happier. And he'd jumped at his chance for freedom, relieved to be away from the torture they constantly inflicted on each other.

But, as he looked around the home that hadn't changed since he'd left, he wondered if this empty kitchen was really better.

Is this happy?

He stopped those thoughts before they went any further. That cold part of himself that didn't care about her happiness, that only cared about creating the life he needed, the dream that had helped him survive their divorce, slid over him, protecting him from any reality he didn't want to see.

She stuck around way after her shift, even went so far as to contemplate sleeping in the front corner booth in order to avoid Gabe.

Maybe he's left, she thought hopefully. She longed for her home, her couch. Her scotch.

Her promise not to drink had evaporated in the heat of Gabe's smile. She needed a drink after today. She'd barked at Trudy—who only ever tried to be kind to her, even when she was a nag—she'd burned her hand and screwed up two tables of food. And now, as penance, she mopped the tiled floor around the stainless steel prep table as if her life depended on it.

Maybe I should not be a chef, she considered. Maybe she could get into the cleaning profession. Work in one of those big high-rises after hours.

She imagined going back to her home and telling Gabe

that she couldn't be his chef because she was making a career change.

She almost laughed thinking about it.

"Alice?" Darnell poked his head out of the back office that adjoined the main prep area. "Can I speak to you a minute?"

She set the mop back in the bucket and propped it against the wall, making sure it wouldn't slip, and stepped into the minuscule manager's office.

"Go ahead and shut the door," Darnell said from behind the cluttered desk. She had to move boxes of recipe and conduct manuals out of the way in order to shut the door that, as long as she'd been here, had never been shut.

She guessed Trudy had tattled. Again.

"Have a seat." He gestured to the one folding chair beneath the giant white board with the schedule on it. She had to move a stack of staff uniforms in order to sit.

"If you wanted me to clean your office, Darnell, you could have just asked." She thought it was a joke, but Darnell didn't laugh. His brown eyes behind the wire-rimmed glasses were stern and a little sad.

Maybe she'd have to up the apology to Trudy. She could buy drinks for the whole staff after work sometime. That should put her back in everyone's good graces.

"What are you doing cleaning the kitchen?" he asked. "Did you, by chance, not notice the staff we have for that?"

"I was just helping out," she said. "I'm a team player."

His mouth dropped open in astonishment for a brief moment, and then he sat back, his chair creaking. "I can only guess you're kidding."

She sighed, pulled off her hairnet and yanked out the clasp that held her hair back. She scratched at her scalp. If she was going to get lectured, she was going to do it in some comfort.

"Do you want to be a chef here?" Darnell asked.

No. "Of course."

"Is that why you show up late, take too many coffee breaks—"

"Everybody does that."

"And order your coworkers around?"

"No, I just do that for fun."

"Trudy doesn't think it's fun," he said through pursed, white lips. "I don't understand why you pick on her. She's the nicest—"

That's why Alice picked on her. Nice made her feel mean. Kindness hurt. "I'll apologize—"

Darnell leaned forward on his desk. "I hired you based on your reputation and the few amazing meals I had at Zinnia." Her gut clenched at the name of her failed restaurant, her baby, her reason for living after Gabe and she ended. "I thought you'd make this franchise something special."

Her mouth fell open and she grabbed a recipe manual from the stack at her knee. "I cook from a manual, Darnell. It's against corporate policy to do something special."

"But you haven't even tried, have you? We have nightly specials and I gave you carte blanche."

"Right, and I've—"

"Served the same thing for two weeks, despite the fact that no one orders it. Our customers don't like duck, Alice. But those ribs you made two months ago were amazing, and you served them for two days. That's it. It's like you don't want to succeed."

Darnell watched her expectantly and Alice dropped her eyes to the recipe manual. She didn't want sympathy. She didn't want to talk about her problems. She wanted to work, pay off the outrageous amount of money she owed the bank and annoy Trudy. That's it.

And drink. Dear God. I need a drink.

"Alice, I don't know the whole story behind what happened at Zinnia—"

"I'll talk to Trudy and I'll put the ribs back up on the specials board." She stood, stared at Darnell with tired eyes. "I have to be back here tomorrow for—"

"No." Darnell shook his head. "You don't."

She slumped.

"You're fired."

Alice's car rolled slowly down Pape and she could see the dim lights, the shadow of someone moving through her kitchen window. She knew it wasn't Charlie.

He's still here, she thought and hit the garage-door opener on her dashboard. An itchy anger chugged through her bloodstream like a drug, making her head spin.

Gabe was the last thing she needed tonight.

The heavy white door lifted and she drove into the parking spot between the empty freezers and the golf clubs Gabe had left. She tried to gather whatever resources were left in her tired, drink-craving, jobless body.

After the day she'd had, there weren't many left. Gabe reentering her life dredged up feelings she'd been managing, longings she'd been subduing.

But tonight those feelings were here in force, like weights on her heart.

I wish I wasn't alone.

I wish I had a family.

And *he* was in there with dim lights and probably tomato soup, something she lost the taste for after he left.

She chewed her beleaguered thumbnail and watched the door between the garage and kitchen as though it might open and Gabe would come running out throwing knives at her car. Not that she was scared of him, just scared of what they were when they were together.

"I don't need anything," she whispered her oft-repeated mantra that eventually got her through the worst days. "There is nothing I want."

But the fates had conspired tonight. Her mortgages—both of them—were due at the end of the week and she had only enough money to cover one.

Am I too old to sell my body? she wondered. But that was a bit drastic, even for her.

She felt raw and panicked, like a trapped animal. Gabe was going to make her an offer she couldn't refuse and she wanted to punish him for it. She wanted him to pay for coming back here and rubbing his success in her face.

She wanted to pick the scabs between them, scratch at old wounds.

I want to fight. Alice smiled, feeling feral. *And there's nothing in this world that Gabe hates more than a fight.*

She opened the door between the garage and the kitchen and Gabe looked up at her from the bread he sliced at her kitchen table. He was too handsome for words in this light.

"You're still here," she said, unbuttoning her dirty chef's whites. "You make yourself at home?"

His smile dimmed a bit, no doubt startled by her biting

sarcasm. She came out swinging, hoping to get a few licks in before he made her that offer and she had to take it.

"Did you take the tour?" she asked, throwing the dirty jacket on the table. "Visit the baby's room?"

His eyes turned to stone. His smile became a grimace.

"Alice." There was that sigh again. It told her, better than words, better than failed doctor's appointments, better than divorce papers, that he was disappointed in her.

And immediately she regretted wanting to fight over this. A fight she never won.

"Alice, there was no baby."

3

"For you," she said, her eyes narrowed like a cat backed into a corner. "That's the problem, isn't it?"

He didn't want to deal with this Alice, the Alice from the end of their marriage. He'd take her cool sarcasm, her judgment and disdain over this Alice—the Alice who wanted to talk about things.

He didn't like this Alice.

"There were no babies, period."

Every fiber in his body, his gut, told him to walk out the door. He didn't have it in him to go another round over this.

She still wallowed in their old misery, he could see it in her black eyes. The miscarriages were all fresh. Real.

"I don't want to talk about this," he said, pushing away the bread. "I'm not here for that."

Her laughter sounded like ice breaking. "Really? And here I thought you finally wanted to sit down and talk—" She pretended to be surprised when he stood.

"This isn't going to work." He slammed the serrated knife onto the small cutting board. "Coming here was a mistake." He grabbed his keys and headed for the front door.

"Ah, the infamous Gabe Mitchell cold shoulder as he heads for the door. How I have missed that." Her sarcasm raked him and suddenly he couldn't get out of there fast enough.

He put his hand on the doorknob and at the same time, she tentatively touched his elbow and a spark of electricity shot up his arm.

"No. Stop. Please, Gabe." Her tone held a certain honesty that he couldn't walk away from. He could walk away from her anger and sarcasm, her lies and evasions. But when she was vulnerable—he just couldn't walk away.

He stopped, his shoulders hunched as if to protect himself. He noticed and immediately straightened.

"I'm—" He could hear her swallow around the words. "I'm sorry. I...forget I said anything."

He weighed the cost of turning around. Of sitting back at that kitchen table, the one from her grandmother.

He needed a chef and she was the best.

He turned and looked right into her liquid black eyes. "No more talk about the marriage or the miscarriages." He shook his head. "It's counterproductive. For both of us."

She huffed a little laugh and licked her lips. "Okay. You're right."

He sat down in the midst of the awkward silence that breathed between them, but he was satisfied that the past wouldn't leap out at him anymore, ambushing his plans for the inn.

"You want something to drink?" she asked, heading for the cabinet above the fridge. She stood on tiptoe and pulled down a bottle of red wine.

And, despite himself, he watched her move. Her pale

skin glowed in the half light. She'd lost some of the lush curvy weight she'd carried in happier days. Her arms were muscled from the hard work of running a kitchen, but the rest of her was a whipcord.

She looked as if she'd missed too many meals. She looked tough.

"I thought you might be hungry," he said. She hadn't even glanced at the stove even though he knew she could smell the tomato soup.

"I ate at work," she said and he didn't force the issue. He'd bet the inn she was lying.

"Wine?" she asked, holding up a bottle.

"I'd love some." He forced himself to be warm to her, cordial. Due to years of practice, he could slip into gracious without batting an eye. It was a suit he donned when he needed it. "I've got Oreos."

That made her smile, and the tension in the room cracked and he could breathe again.

"I met your roommate," Gabe said, watching her uncork the bottle like a professional. "Nice guy."

He tried to steer the conversation toward her situation, remind them both, no matter how unsavory, they needed each other.

"He's clean and pays the rent on time."

"Sounds like the proper arrangement. How was work?"

"Why don't we just cut to the chase here, Gabe."

She popped the cork, poured a perfect four ounces in each glass, grabbed a cookie from the package on the table, then retreated across the kitchen. She hoisted herself onto the counter, sitting in the shadows. He could only see the gleam of her skin, the shine of her eyes and her shaking hands as she lifted her glass to her mouth and drank like a woman in need.

Again, his gut told him to get out of that kitchen, away from the quicksand of Alice's pain.

"Go ahead, Gabe," she said. "Give me your pitch."

He rubbed his face, wondering how he'd ended up here, of all places.

"Having second thoughts?" she asked, her voice a sarcastic coo from the darkness by the stove. "Wondering if your ex-wife might be drinking a bit too much? Thinking maybe she's just a little too much trouble?"

"Yep," he told her point-blank. She poured herself another glass, not even trying to assuage his fears.

"Well, you had to be pretty damn desperate to come find me. So unless things have changed since this afternoon, you're still pretty damn desperate, right?"

He nodded.

"Let me tell you, drunk or not, I'm still the best chef you know. So, give me your pitch."

"I can't ask you to do this if you're...not stable."

"I'm plenty stable, Gabe. I just drink too much after work. I drink too much so I can live in this house and not go crazy."

He understood that all too well, but it wasn't enough. He couldn't jeopardize the Riverview Inn with a bad decision, and Alice could be a very bad decision.

"But Zinnia? What happened there?"

"I didn't realize I was applying for a job. You came to me."

"Yeah, I came to you in a parking lot at Johnny O's. You're the best chef I know, but something's happened to you and I think I need to know before I make you an offer."

"I'll worry about me, you worry about your inn." She stared unflinchingly into his eyes and he knew from years of hard experience that he wouldn't get any more from her.

"I could leave," he said, a warning he knew he really couldn't follow through on.

"You have before," she said. "But I think you're too desperate to walk out that door and—" her smile was wan "—I'm too desperate to let you. Tell me what the job is."

Honesty again, when he'd least expected it, and as usual when she was real with him, he couldn't refuse.

"The position is executive chef at Riverview Inn. Opening day is May 1."

She choked on her Oreo. "That's a month away. Cutting it close, don't you think?"

"No one knows that better than me right now." He smiled ruefully. "As bad as that sounds it's actually worse. I have the Crimpson wedding in June and—"

"Crimpson? Crimpson frozen foods?" she asked and he nodded. "Well, that's quite a feather in your cap."

"Right, so it's pretty important that the event be flawless."

"Two months?" she asked. She leaned over the stove and waved the scent of the soup up to her nose. "Opening day in four weeks and a wedding in eight?"

"After the event you can walk away," he told her. "And I imagine it would be best if you did."

She dipped her pinkie in the red liquid and touched it to her tongue. "I imagine it would, too." She hopped down from the counter and opened the cupboard to the left of the gas stove. She sprinkled the soup with balsamic vinegar and a couple of twists from the black-pepper grinder and tasted again. She nodded, so he guessed it was better.

"Staff?" she asked.

Gabe didn't answer and her black eyes pinned him to the wall. "Staff?" she repeated.

"A young guy with some excellent past experience."

Gabe watched the wine in his glass instead of meeting her eyes and hoped that kid who'd been fired from McDonald's could be trusted around knives and headstrong chefs.

"I'll need more," she said.

"You going to take the job?"

"Not so fast," she said, pulling down the kosher salt from the cupboard and giving the soup a few hefty pinches. "What are you going to pay me?"

He braced himself. "Twenty—"

"Nope."

"You'll only be there two months."

"I won't be there at all for twenty grand."

"Okay." He sighed, having expected that. His budget for a far less experienced chef was forty grand for the year. He was blowing everything on this gamble—he'd have to take money from the landscaping funds to pay another chef when she left. "Thirty. For two months' work, I won't give you more."

She tasted the soup again, nodded definitively and took it off the burner.

"Are you going to have any?" Gabe asked, gesturing to the heavy pot.

"Nope. And I won't go to your inn for thirty grand, either."

"Thirty-five and some shares in the place."

Her eyes burned fever bright. He knew what shares represented. Income. Success. And after two months she wouldn't have to work for it.

It would help, maybe after they split ways again. Make it so she wouldn't have to work at a terrible job or share her house with a stranger.

"You know it's a good deal. I've never had a restaurant not turn a profit."

She rubbed her forehead and he knew he had her. It was just a matter of sealing the deal.

"It would be a fresh start, Al."

Her nickname warmed the air.

"It hardly seems fresh." She laughed. "You're my ex-husband and this is an old plan of ours. It feels like trouble."

"I couldn't agree more." He laughed, too. "But you'd have total run of the kitchen."

She scoffed. "Right."

"I'm serious, I'll be very busy—"

"Getting in my way." She looked at him for a brief moment and all the problems in their relationship—the fights and clashing egos—for some reason, in this room with the wine, he felt...nostalgic for them. Those nights when he made her so mad she threw things at him, broke plates against the floor and ruined meals with her temper. The long days when he wouldn't talk to her, giving her a silent treatment so cold and deep that the only way to thaw both of them...

She cleared her throat, seeming uncomfortable, as if she'd been thinking the same thing. "I'll do it."

Gabe felt both jubilant and wary. *Is this the right thing? Am I making a deal with the devil?* "I'm so glad."

"But—" she held up a finger "—I'm out of there the second that wedding is over and I run the kitchen. Not you."

He nodded, stood and held out his hand.

"I'm serious, Gabe. I won't have you trying to take things over. You hired me to be executive chef—"

"I promise." He put his hand on his chest and bowed his head slightly. "I absolutely promise to stay out of your way as long as you promise to try to be a team player. My dad and Max—"

"Your dad and Max are there?" she asked, bright joy filtering through the dark clouds on her face.

"They are and they'll be very glad to see you."

She smiled and held out her hand. "I can be a team player."

"And I can stay out of your way."

They shook on it and Gabe had to wonder who was going to break their promise first.

4

Patrick Mitchell watched his oldest son walk away whistling.

Whistling! And after the bomb Gabe had just laid on them, watching him whistle was akin to watching him hit himself in the head with a ball-peen hammer.

"Alice?" Patrick, incredulous, turned to his youngest son. "Max? Alice was your idea?"

Max ignored him, or pretended to, and poured more eggshell paint in the trays. He practiced being oblivious as though there was a contest.

"Son." Patrick tried again as Max dipped his roller in the paint and began applying their last coat on the last wall of the kitchen. "I leave you alone with him for ten minutes and this is what you do? Are you trying to ruin this inn?"

"He needed a chef." Max shrugged, but there was a smile on his lips. "Alice is a chef."

Patrick nodded. "She is, sure. But she's also pure trouble for that boy."

"I thought you liked Alice," Max said.

"I do. I love her like a daughter but they are trouble for each other and she is the last thing your brother needs."

"Please." Max looked at him out of the corner of his eye, but still that devil's smile was on his lips. If the situation weren't so dire, Patrick would be happy to see Alice. "They're grown-ups. They can make it work. At least we'll eat well while she's here. I'm about a week away from liver failure after eating your cooking for the past few months."

Patrick's mouth dropped open. "Where did I go wrong?" He pretended to be upset, when really these past few months had been the happiest of his life. This teasing was their old shtick. Kept them from ever having to address anything head-on—such as emotion. Such as the past. "I'm supposed to be growing senile on a porch somewhere with grandkids on my knee. Not working manual labor for one son and roommates with the other."

"Right, because living with my dad is exactly what I want to be doing," Max said without heat, and Patrick yearned, absolutely longed, to ask his boy what had happened to him. What was wrong. What was still hurting him so badly from the shooting last year that sent him into this tailspin. It wasn't as though he was that different—the scar on his neck was new, sure. But he still laughed. He still made every effort to get the best of his brother. But it was as though he did those things because he was supposed to, not because he wanted to. Something had happened to leach the joy out of his boy, and he wanted to know what that was.

But if he asked, Max would probably fall on the floor in heart failure or shock. The Mitchell men didn't ask probing questions.

So, they worked, the way they always did, instead of saying the important things. And Patrick hoped that whatever Max needed he was getting in some way.

The back door to the kitchen opened, letting in a warm breeze and a shaft of bright spring sunlight.

A woman stood in the doorway but it wasn't Alice. The woman didn't give off the kinetic energy that had surrounded his daughter-in-law.

Ex-daughter-in-law.

"Excuse me?" she said, stepping from the bright doorway into the kitchen. The door shut behind her and her features emerged from silhouette. "I'm looking for the chef." She had a pretty smile that turned her plain face into something quite lovely.

"She's not here," Max said.

And his dumb son watched the paint dry in front of him rather than look at the pretty girl to his left.

Patrick despaired for the boy, he really did.

"She's supposed to be here Monday," Max said. He darted a quick look her way, then returned to the careful application of a second coat of pale cream paint on a pale cream wall, as though failure could blow up the building.

"Maybe there's something we could do for you?" Patrick asked, stepping into the breach.

"Well, is Gabe—"

"Hello?" Gabe ducked his head out of the small office he'd built off the kitchen. "Hi!" He caught sight of the woman and Patrick knew his eldest son would appreciate how she appeared plain but somehow interesting all the same. True to form, Gabe smiled, the old charmer, and shook the woman's hand. "I'm Gabe."

Patrick shot Max a look that said, "That's how you do it, nincompoop." Max just rolled his eyes.

"I'm Daphne from Athens Organics. We talked briefly on the phone yesterday. I was hoping to meet with your chef about being a supplier for your kitchen."

"Of course," Gabe said, "My chef isn't here yet, but I'm so glad you stopped by. Come on into my office." He opened the door for her and she smiled girlishly and Max rolled his eyes again.

Silence filled the kitchen after Gabe shut the office door. Patrick watched his son paint and Max ignored him.

"You're a virgin, aren't you?" Patrick asked.

"Shut up, Dad."

"It's the only thing that explains why you're such an idiot around women."

"I'm not an idiot, I'm just not...Gabe. And that's fine by me." He smiled, that sharp, wicked smile from the corner of his mouth. It made Patrick feel as though the boy he remembered with the temper and the laugh that could light up a room was still in there somewhere. "And it's pretty okay by the women I have sex with, too."

"Thank God."

Max laughed, sort of. And Patrick's heart leaped.

Now, he wondered. *Is now the right time?* The letter he'd been carrying in the front chest pocket of his work shirt felt like deadweight against his chest. At night, it sat on his bedside table and glowed with a life of its own.

He couldn't sleep. He didn't eat. He took a hundred bathroom breaks a day so he could sit down and reread the words he'd memorized.

The office door opened and Gabe and Daphne stepped back into the kitchen. Her color was high and her smile ready as they shook hands. Gabe walked her out the door to her car.

"Maybe he's going to start working on those grandkids you want," Max said, nodding in the direction his brother had gone. "It's about time, the guy's been thinking about a family since he could walk."

I just want them to know love. To know love like I knew it, is that so hard? Patrick wondered. *So impossible?*

The subject of love was a sore one among the Mitchell men. Had been since Iris walked out on them thirty years ago.

Not that he was counting.

"You know—" he dipped his paintbrush into the can of paint he'd set on the top step of the ladder and watched Max for a reaction "—when you lost your mother—"

"Dad." Max practically growled the word. "What is this new fascination with Mom? You haven't mentioned her in years and now every time I turn around you're bringing her up."

"Maybe it's because I'm living with her son, who is just as moody and muleheaded as she was."

Max fell silent. Any reminder of being like his mother could turn him off like a light switch.

"When you lost her—"

"You make it sound like she died!" Max cried, finally setting the roller down. "Or like we misplaced her somewhere. She left. She walked away. I don't want to talk about her. If you want to reminisce about the past, talk to Gabe."

Gabe had given him the same reaction every time he tried talking about Iris. Patrick couldn't blame them—Iris had walked away from them, which, as Gabe had told him, was worse than if she'd died.

She didn't want us, Dad. She didn't want any of us, he'd said.

It wasn't true—entirely. She had wanted them, but there had been things happening that the boys were too young to understand or remember. They didn't understand why Patrick didn't just get over it. Over her.

He'd held out a thin ribbon of hope that maybe, just maybe Iris would realize she'd made a mistake and she'd forgive his. Ignore his foolish anger and pride. For years he'd held on to that ribbon. Two weeks ago she'd finally picked up her end.

5

M onday morning Alice opened the kitchen door of the Riverview Inn and stepped into a dream. Her dream.

Doubt, second thoughts, worry that she'd somehow screw this up the way she'd screwed up Zinnia, had plagued her for the past three days, since taking the job. Uncertainty had dogged her as she drove down from Albany. But now, as she set down her bag and tried to catch her breath, worry vanished.

This kitchen was hers. Meant to be hers. It was as if Gabe had opened her head and pulled out the daydreams and plans she'd been accumulating over the years.

A south-facing window overlooking a brilliant green forest filled the room with sunshine. The pale cream walls seemed to glow in the clear morning light and the appliances sparkled, clean and unused.

Racks of pots hung from the ceiling. She reached up and carefully knocked the saucepan into a sauté pan and reflected light scattered across the far wall.

It was the most beautiful kind of chandelier.

A stainless steel table filled the bottom portion of the L-shaped room beside two big glass-front refrigerators.

In a place that was often busy and loud and filled with a sort of graceful chaos, the silence of the downtimes seemed almost healing.

A kitchen at rest, a kitchen such as this one, was a beautiful thing. A place of peace.

She ran her hand along the chopping block sitting next to the stove. The same monster slab of oak, easily ten inches thick, used to sit in their house. It had come from Gabe's mother whose parents had been Polish butchers. Thousands of pigs had been bled on that wood, thousands of cabbages had been chopped, thousands of perogies had been rolled and formed there. Alice wanted to climb on top of it and dance.

This kitchen even smelled like a fresh start.

I will stop drinking, she promised. *I will not waste this chance.* She made the promise even as the remainder of last night's wine throbbed in her skull. *I will swallow my resentment and try very hard not to fight with my ex-husband.*

"Hey," Gabe said from behind her as if her promise had conjured him. She couldn't quite face him yet. Things in her were shaken loose by the beauty of the place, by her earnest desire to deserve this fresh start.

"Executive chef," she said, opening a door to find a small closet, lined with shelves, ready for spices and root vegetables, maple syrup and vinegars, "reporting for duty."

"What do you think?" he asked and she finally had to look at him. For an instant she wanted to shield her eyes from the radiant brightness of him. He was clean and fresh in a wrinkled white shirt and khaki pants, his blond hair mussed by his hands, his face tanned from working outside.

He looked like a lifeguard. A Swiss Alps ski-rescue guy. He just needed the dog.

She felt small in comparison, dark and mean, dressed in black because it didn't require her to think to coordinate.

"Alice?" he said, breaking in to her ugly comparisons. He ducked his head to look into her eyes and smiled. "What do you think? Recognize it?"

She realized, belatedly, that the kitchen wasn't a coincidence. She'd told him a million times what a kitchen should look like according to her. She'd sketched the floor plan on the bare skin of his back over and over again.

"It's amazing," she said, her joy in finding her dream brought to life turning to cold resentment. Of course he would take this for himself, too. "You know that."

"I practically have the floor plan tattooed on my back." He grinned and the reminder of their intimacies, casually uttered out loud, chilled her to the bone. "When the time came to design the kitchen, I just remembered everything you taught me."

It was a compliment, probably a sincere one, but she didn't want compliments.

This is not mine, she told herself, ripping the dream from her clenched fists. *I am hired help. I am a bit player.* She had no business coveting the butcher's block, imagining years of early mornings in this kitchen, planning menus.

There is nothing I want, she reminded herself. *There is nothing I need.*

She forced cold distance into her head and her heart and when she looked at the beautiful kitchen, the chandelier of pots and pans, she just saw *things*. Inanimate objects that had no relationship to her, that cost her nothing and only represented a way to get out of debt and move on with her life.

They were tools. That's all. Gabe, this kitchen, the whole inn, they were a means to an end.

"I think we better get to work if you want to open in a month," she said, cold as ice.

"But did you see the view?" Gabe pointed to the window. "Come on, we can have coffee and take a walk around the grounds. We have a capacity of one hundred guests between the cottages and the lodge, which we're hoping—"

"No." She shook her head. "I just want to work, Gabe. That's all."

For a moment she thought he might ask her what was wrong. Instead, true to form, he nodded in that definitive way that always indicated he was biting his tongue. "Okay. Come on into the office and we'll talk—"

"Get your hands off me!" someone yelled, and both Gabe and Alice whirled to the doorway leading to the dining room. They stood like deer in headlights while the swinging door banged open and Max and a teenage boy plowed into the kitchen. "Didn't you hear what I said!" The kid, practically drowning in oversize black clothes, yelled.

"Yep. And I'm not touching you."

"Good, don't start."

Alice nearly stepped back, as though the kid were a rabid dog.

"Here he is," Max said and from the corner of her eye she saw Gabe's mouth fall open.

"You're kidding me," he said.

"Nope." Max shook his head. "This is Cameron."

"Cut that out, man," Cameron said, jerking himself away from Max. "The name is DJ Dolla Dolla Bills."

"That makes you sound like an idiot," Max said. "Your name is Cameron."

"Hi, Max," Alice said, pleased to see her former brother-in-law. The best things about Gabe were his brother and father, both as emotionally stunted as Gabe, but at least they didn't try to pretend otherwise.

"Hey, Alice," Max said with a quick grin. "Good to see you."

"Good to see you, too." She meant it. "How you keeping?"

"Starving," he said. "We've been living on toast and freeze-dried noodles around here."

Alice shuddered and Max's grin stretched into a smile. He looked thin, painfully so, and wounded in some dark way, as if all the intensity that had illuminated him was banked, burning out.

"What the hell am I doing here, man?" Cameron asked. "This is an after-school program."

"Not when you've got a day off school. Then it's an all-day program." Max answered.

"This your love-child you never told us about?" Alice asked Max, falling into their old give-and-take.

"This dude ain't my father," Cameron answered for him.

"Gabe didn't tell you?" Max asked, his dark eyebrows hitting his hairline, and Alice suddenly felt a serious lack of information.

"Tell me what?" She crossed her arms over her chest, just in case Gabe misinterpreted her tone as happy.

It took a moment, but Gabe finally issued a response. He looked at her, put on his game face and said, "He's your staff."

"Bullshit!" the kid yelled.

Alice laughed. "I'm with him."

Gabe winced and remained silent, which could mean only one thing. Alice's mouth fell open. "You're kidding."

He shook his head.

"You're kidding." She turned to Max, who only shrugged.

She finally focused on the kid, whose eyes met hers briefly. "I got nothing to kid about," he said, looking as unhappy as she felt.

She shook her head. "I can work alone until I get proper staff."

"Okay," Max said, opening the swing door behind him. "Let's go back to stacking that wood."

"This is bullshit!" The kid hollered as Max led him into the dining room.

Gabe's silence worried her, actually set small stones a-twirl in her stomach. "What aren't you telling me, Gabe?"

"There's no money for staff unless you take a pay cut," he said point-blank. "Not until the next check comes in from the Crimpsons."

"When will that be?" She asked, disbelieving.

"Two weeks."

"Even if that kid was Cordon Bleu trained, I couldn't pull together the menu for this wedding with one staff member!"

"I know." He rubbed his forehead. "We open in a month and I've already got some reservations and am running an Internet spring promotion, so I should get more. I can make this work. We can use the money—"

She laughed, listening to him rob from Peter to pay Paul.

"You think this is funny?" he asked, his blue eyes danger-ously clouded over.

"A little, yeah."

"Great. Wonderful attitude from my chef."

"You hired a chef, Gabe. Not a cheer-leader. If you're screwing up—"

Her comment must have lit his dormant temper because he bristled. "I'm not screwing up. You're the one doing two

months' work for the price of what I had earmarked for a
yearly chef's salary."

She shrugged. "You should have gotten a beginner chef."

"No, you should have been reasonable."

"Ah, I thought I recognized that voice."

Patrick Mitchell's loud voice boomed through the
kitchen, stalling their argument as he stepped in from the
outside. His red flannel shirt matched his ruddy cheeks and
it was as if the sun had come out from behind clouds.
Indomitably cheerful, that was Patrick, and she was inordi-
nately glad to see him.

"There's only one person Gabe actually fights with,"
Patrick said and held out his thick burly arms. Alice allowed
herself to be hugged, the sensation odd but pleasant enough
since it didn't last too long.

When was the last time someone touched me? she
wondered. Even casually. That awkward embarrassing kiss
from Charlie months ago, when she'd been so lonely and
sad and drunk that she'd let him touch her.

She didn't know when she lost the capacity for casual
touch, when any sort of physical affection, no matter how
benign, made her ache.

"How is my favorite former daughter-in-law?" Patrick
asked, his blue eyes twinkling.

Some of the tension from locking horns with Gabe fell
away and she smiled, even patted Patrick's grizzled cheek.

"Don't tell me he's got you working here, too?" she asked.

"Unpaid labor." Patrick shook his head, always one for
teasing. "At least now we'll have decent chow."

"Don't be too sure, Dad," Gabe said, leaning against the
doorjamb of his office. "She may have decided she doesn't
like the terms."

"Always trying to make it my fault, aren't you, Gabe."

"If the shoe—"

"Wonderful!" Patrick rubbed his hands together. "If you don't mind, Max and I are just going to pull up some chairs and watch you two duke it out for the next few months. That way no work will get done." His eyes flicked from her to Gabe, who, chagrined by his father's reverse chastisement, looked down at his shoes.

"I told Max this was going to be trouble," Patrick said and she could feel his direct gaze on her face.

She'd only been here minutes and already things were going wrong.

"I can make it work," Gabe said, resolute. "It won't be a problem."

"For you," she said.

"You, either," Gabe insisted, his tone hard, his smile sharp. "I will make it work."

She nodded, wondering why she felt so small. So dark and ill-tempered. He was the one who had lied, who had told her he had staff. She shouldn't feel bad because she was making him hold up his end of the bargain.

"You always do," she said. He did. He could make gold out of hay without making it look hard.

"Ah, that's how children should play," Patrick said. "Nice."

"Don't you have some work to do, Dad?" Gabe asked.

"I'm going to hook up your fancy dishwasher," he said, pointing to the far corner of the room where a dishwasher sat, with its tube and wire guts spread out across the floor.

He winked at Alice and vanished behind the equipment.

"Let's get to work," she said and pushed past Gabe into his minuscule office. "I've got some ideas for menus."

Gabe had prepared himself for the worst. He was forti-
fied by too much caffeine, and ready to do battle with Alice
over kitchen operations. But, surprisingly, there was no
battle. It didn't take long for them to ease into their old
routine. They were rusty at first, but the one thing they'd
always shared—well, two things—was that they were both
perfectionists. Fortunately, they both had the same idea of
what perfect was.

"All right—" Alice looked down at her notebook "—
breakfast buffets at the beginning. You have some kind of
waitstaff, or do you expect me to do that?" She glanced at
him from beneath her lashes and her eyes, black as night,
twinkled just a little more than they had before, and he
sighed.

"I've got staff."

"Juvenile delinquents?" She was having too much fun
with this at his expense. "DJ Dolla Dolla Bills going to be
your front-of-house staff? He'll be a real hit with guests."

"You're hilarious. No, I've got it taken care of. Keep going
—" He pointed at her list, though he had all the pertinent
details of their conversation locked in his head. His years as
a waiter had honed his memory.

"Two options for lunch. Two options for dinner,
including a vegetarian pasta, and three desserts." She
tapped her pencil on the pad. "Are there going to be kids?"
she asked but she didn't look up. He wondered how long
that open emotional sore of hers was going to still bleed.

"There are no reservations with children yet. I'll let you
know when there are."

"Great." She took a deep breath, her thin shoulders

lifting under her black blouse. "Then I can make up something kid friendly."

"I'm missing some equipment," he told her. "Food processor, blender, some larger roasting pans. If you want to write up a list I'll go see what I can find."

"I brought what I'll need," she said, still staring at the pad of paper. "It's in my car."

"Always prepared." He repeated fondly the motto she used to live by. The woman used to carry a can opener, a bottle opener, a paring knife and curry powder in the glove box of her car.

Camping with her had been like roughing it at the Ritz.

She flashed him a quick smile but never stopped scribbling.

"I'm getting a list of food we're going to need. I can run to Athens today and pick up some stuff," she said, more to herself than him.

"I've found a few organic farms in the area."

"Great. Let me just finish this…"

She still appeared so dramatic, her thinness only adding somehow to the tragic appeal of her.

Daphne of Athens Organics, her wholesome, honest plainness was the exact opposite of his ex-wife. In fact, most of the women he'd dated after the marriage ended could be considered, in one way or another, the exact opposite of Alice.

Which wasn't an accident.

"Now, the organic farmers. What are we looking at?"

"I met with a local farmer yesterday and we have an appointment to tour her farm tomorrow morning." He handed Alice Daphne's card.

"*We?*" Alice asked and exhaled heavily. "Gabe, you are

supposed to be staying out of my way, remember? We shook on it."

"Okay." He nodded and leaned forward in his chair, putting his pencil against the top edge of his blotter, reluctant to look at her. *Why?* he wondered, angry with himself. *It's been five years, I've dated a lot of women and I'm sure she went on her share of dates, too.* But still, it seemed like he might shatter this nice...equilibrium between them.

"You have an appointment," he said. "I...have a date."

He cleared his throat to break the silence.

"You're dating a farmer?" she asked. She blinked at him, unruffled. He couldn't tell if she was kidding with him, which would be like the old Alice. But this new incarnation...she didn't seem to be much for joking.

"Her name is Daphne and she runs the farm."

"So, she's a farmer."

"She runs...yes, she's a farmer."

"You date her in the morning?" she asked.

"It's our first. For coffee." Why he felt compelled to tell her, he wasn't sure. But perhaps it was better to get it all out there, instead of having her be surprised at some point. A surprised Alice was a recipe for the unexpected.

"This should be good," she said, her lips quirked in a grin. She stood, tucked her notebook into her bag.

That's it? he wondered, waiting for her punch line. Her zinger. But none seemed forthcoming and he wondered if maybe he'd braced himself for nothing. Maybe, he realized with a slight relaxing of his shoulders, they could do this—work together, be in each other's lives—like adults.

"You want to show me to my room, or cabin or whatever?" she asked. Her eyes held no secrets. No questions, no suppressed anger and resentment.

He nodded and stood up as well.

We're going to be just fine, he thought and grabbed the key to the smallest cabin that so far was unrented.

The need for a drink was stronger than all her promises and wishes. The need to drink was a demon in the back of her throat, in the back of her head, howling and screaming and tearing her apart with temptation.

A date. Of course. Gabe dates. She knew that intellectually. But to have to watch him do it made her feel trapped.

She followed her ex-husband out the back door of the kitchen, around the front of the inn and down a narrow foot-worn path and battled her demon with the cooling calming influence of lists.

Lists of men she'd dated since her divorce.

Marcus, Luke and...

Marcus and Luke. Each for about ten minutes.

That was depressing. Fine. She'd focus on work lists. Things she needed for work.

Well, first on the list was calling Daphne and rescheduling her appointment. Alice wasn't going to drive up to the farm with Gabe for his *date*. She needed to find a dairy supplier. Meats. Start making stocks, pesto—

"Here you go," Gabe said, opening the door to a cabin. "This is yours until I need to rent it and then I'll move you into the lodge with Dad and Max and myself. Cleaning staff will come by once a week with fresh linens and towels."

The cabin was small, sweet and redolent of the scent of fresh paint and sawdust. The blue and green linens on the white-painted brass bed lifted and waved in the cross

breeze between the open east-facing windows and the
door.

The cabin was exactly as Gabe had always envisioned
for his inn. *His* dream come true. Her throat tightened with
uncomfortable emotion.

"Bathroom's through there." He pointed behind the
door, then handed her the keys.

She took them, clenching her fingers around the cool
metal. *Say something*, she urged herself. *Say something about
how well he's done. How perfectly he's brought the dream to life,
how glad I am to see this come to fruition. Say something.
Anything.*

"Shout if you need anything," Gabe said, then turned
and walked away.

She watched him go, the words dead in her throat.
Another in a long line of missed opportunities.

Unpacking her personal stuff from the car took an
embarrassingly small amount of time. Four chef jackets, two
pairs of checkered pants, some regular clothes and clogs.

She shook her head at the meager clothes hanging in
the closet, like deflated, lonely people.

Toothbrush, expensive face and hand lotion sat on the
glass shelf over the old-fashioned pedestal sink in the
bathroom.

She took a look around the cozy cabin that was no doubt
made for lovers, for two toothbrushes and closets filled with
his-and-her clothes, and shuddered.

I gotta get the hell out of here.

Far more comfortable in the kitchen, she unloaded those indispensable kitchen items from her house. Food processor, standing mixer, her knives, her grandmother's cast iron skillet, roasting pans and recipe box—all handed down in her family like diamond engagement rings were handed down in others.

With nothing else to do but tour the grounds and constantly come face-to-face with the physical reality of their once-shared dream, she pulled out the Athens Organics card and rescheduled her appointment.

"Well," she said when Daphne asked her for a good time to reschedule. It was five in the afternoon. "I'm free right now. I can be there in a half hour."

"Ahh," Daphne stalled for a moment and Alice wondered if she actually was going to have to piggyback Gabe's coffee date.

Really, she wondered, *was there anything more depressing.*

"That work's great," Daphne finally said. "I also have some information on local butchers and a great recommendation for an organic dairy farm near Coxsackie."

Smart woman, Alice thought, hanging up. *But I'm still not going to like her.*

Alice grabbed her keys and beat a hasty retreat from Riverview Inn.

She flew down the New York interstate then took Highway 12 along the river, past Black Rock and the old Van Loan mansion. Twilight came to the Catskills like a slow bleed of India ink from the east, while the western sky remained light behind the rounded back of the old mountain chain.

It was beautiful country. She'd grown up here—her parents were only a hundred miles away from where Gabe had built the inn.

Alice rolled down the window and let the cool air hit her

cheek, slide into the open neck of her blouse. She was tired, hungry but, she was honest enough to admit it... excited. Excited about filling the back of her car with herbs and organic potatoes and radishes. Excited about waking up early tomorrow, putting on a pot of coffee and getting to work.

Excited about organic dairy suppliers, mint pesto, incoming guests...all of it. She was excited about life again. She'd lived in such a small dark place for so long, constantly trying to fill up the emptiness in herself with empty things—work she didn't care about, wine that didn't help her forget. But this opportunity...she felt flushed with ideas.

She cranked the wheel left, nearly missing the turnoff to the farm. Another quarter mile and she was in front of a lovely white and yellow farmhouse. Dogs ran out from bushes to greet her and she felt, inexplicably, that Athens Organics was going to be a perfect match for her kitchen.

"Hi."

Alice turned to find a young blond girl standing at her window. She was about five.

For one second, one naked and vulnerable moment, Alice couldn't breathe.

Alice didn't even have to do the math or work hard to recall the expected due date of her first pregnancy. The information was imprinted on her bones. She knew that her own daughter, stillborn at twenty weeks would be this girl's age.

"Hi," she said and swallowed. "I'm Alice—"

"You're here to see my mom," the girl said. "She's out in the herb field and I'm supposed to take you there." She smiled. Her front tooth was missing, and something purple and sticky was stuck to the side of her face.

"Your mom is Daphne?" Alice asked needlessly, knowing the answer already because fate was just that vindictive.

"Yep." The girl nodded, blond pigtails flapping with her zeal. "I'm Helen."

Alice climbed out of her car on legs that felt weak around the knees. She was used to seeing children, little girls or boys who were the age of her two babies who never made it would be. She was used to talking with them, trying not stare at them too long or touch them at all. And she was quick to leave their company.

She just wasn't used to meeting the children of women Gabe planned to date.

No wonder, she thought cruelly, as those parts of her that had begun to feel full—her joy, excitement and thrill—emptied again in her unrelenting grief. *No wonder he's ready to date the farmer.*

Two hours later, won over by Daphne's farm and exhausted by trying to ignore Helen, Alice parked in the area behind the kitchen that was still covered in grass. She leaped out of the car, leaving the herbs and sample produce in the back. She'd return for it after she got dinner made.

It was late already, seven-thirty, so she quickly took stock of what the men had been living on.

Bacon, eggs, pasta. Cream for Patrick's coffee. Two wizened apples, an inexplicable lime and two industrial-size cans of coffee.

All signs pointed to pasta cabonara. With nothing green in sight. The produce in the back of her car was earmarked for the work in the morning. Besides, vegetable-free was the way the Mitchell men liked their dinners.

She pulled down the new pans, turned the dials on the gas stove, and soon, the smell of bacon and garlic sautéing in olive oil had attracted the men like bees to a picnic.

Gabe came in first, standing in the doorway watching her until her hands felt clumsy, her whole body flushed with awareness.

"Thank God," Max said as he came in, grabbed a beer and headed into the dining room.

"You are a blessing, a real blessing," Patrick said, kissing her cheek and actually succeeding in making Alice blush. "I'll set out the plates." He grabbed the classic white dishes Gabe had picked out.

Soon, it was just the smell of bacon, her, Gabe at the door and the heat of blood in her face that would not go away.

She wondered if he knew that Daphne had a daughter. If he'd done the math and realized that the little girl was the same age theirs would have been.

She doubted it. Not that he knew about the girl, that she was sure of—of course he'd date women who'd proved their love of family, their ability to create one—he just wouldn't have done the math.

"Go sit down," she finally said when she couldn't tolerate his observation anymore. "I'll bring it out."

"About tomorrow morning—"

"I've already gone," she interrupted. "We met this afternoon. She'll be a fantastic supplier and she gave me great sources for organic meats and dairy."

She's a wonderful mother with a funny great kid, I imagine you'll share a long and happy life with a million children running around.

I need a drink.

"You've jumped in with both feet." Gabe smiled. "It's still your first day."

She shrugged. "You hired me to work."

He stepped past her and she could feel him at her back though there was at least five feet between them. "It's good to have you here," he said, his voice that warm dark purr that turned her insides soft. "Max actually laughed like he meant it. Dad nearly fell out of his chair."

She dumped the dried pasta into the boiling water and didn't say anything for fear of saying too much. She put butter in the frying pan, studiously not looking at Gabe, pretending to be casual when it felt as if her head would explode.

Still he didn't leave, he stood at the door like a sentinel.

"Are you going to eat with us?" he asked.

She shook her head, there was only so far a woman could go in a day and she'd hit her limit. "Lots of work to do," she lied.

"I didn't think so," he said, knowing her so well she nearly dropped the cream container right into the sauce.

And finally, just as she thought she might scream from the tension, he left.

6

It was late and the demons riding her wouldn't back down. In fact, as Alice tried to deep breathe through her cravings, think of all the things she had in her life that she could screw up by drinking, the demons bit harder into her spine, eating at it until she had no defense against her need.

Her grandmother's recipes had been sorted and resorted; the ones that fit her idea of inn fare had been culled. The dinner dish she'd brought to the cabin from the kitchen was clean and upside down in her small shower.

She'd paced. She'd made lists and notes. She'd called Charlie on her cell phone to check on Felix.

Ten o'clock and it was just her and the demons.

Gabe won't like it. You might lose this job. You might have to go back to the city and find some other job you can't stand. You have an early morning. Lots of work to do.

She watched the moon rise from the small window in her bathroom, cupped her shaking hands under the silver light, let it bathe her face like clean cold water.

There is nothing I want, there is nothing—

"Just something to get me to sleep," she finally whispered to no one, her spine gone, her will devoured by demons.

She stepped out into the cool air of spring in the Catskills, zipped up her maroon fleece and went looking for Max and Patrick, who, she was betting her sanity, would have a bottle somewhere.

The lodge glowed, the windows of the dining room revealing mellow light and a fire in the fireplace. It looked warm, welcoming, a beautiful beacon in the night.

But it was all wasted on her.

Drink. Drink. Drink.

She pulled open the heavy oak doors, leaning with all her weight just so she could slide in and catch the tail end of Patrick's laughter as it reverberated across pine and within cathedral ceilings.

"Swans?" Max snorted. "You've got to be kidding me."

The three of them sat around the fire on brass-studded burgundy leather couches. Patrick and Gabe held tumblers filled with a promising amber liquid. Max had a beer.

"Hi," she said, her eyes on the bottle of Jim Beam on the coffee table next to their feet. The three of them turned to find her in the shadows, each registering varying degrees of pleasure at seeing her.

She concentrated on Patrick and the bottle, though she could feel Gabe there, at the edge of the light, touched by shadows.

"Well, if it isn't our chef." Patrick's big voice boomed. "Come sit. Have a drink."

He pulled himself out of his deep seat and walked over to the wooden bar in the corner to grab her a glass.

Hurry. Hurry. Hurry.

Her hungry eyes followed him until she felt the burning touch of Gabe's gaze on her face.

She turned, met those eyes and saw what she knew would be there. A question. Worry. For him. For her. A profound wish that she wouldn't drink what Patrick poured for her.

She almost laughed.

Patrick poured her a splash of whiskey and gestured to the empty seat beside Max, who toasted her with his beer.

"Good dinner tonight," he said. "Best thing I've eaten in months."

"You're in sad shape if that's the case," she said, forcing herself not to gulp down her drink.

She took a sip, sighed and stretched out her legs, imitating someone having a casual drink, enjoying the moment rather than counting the seconds between sips.

"So?" she said, looking around at the silent, masculine faces. "Are we having a staff meeting? Should Max go get Cameron?"

"Nope, just trying to work out the details for the wedding," Gabe said.

Max, beside her, chuckled before taking another swig of beer.

"Must be good," she said.

"I don't know if you could say good," Gabe cringed. The firelight hit his face, highlighting those things about his features that she'd always loved. His slightly too big nose which was balanced by his hard jawline and his ridiculously long eyelashes, a beautiful surprise on such a masculine face. The small scar on his right cheek from an evening of oysters and too much wine, when he'd gotten overzealous with the oyster knife.

He turned to her, no doubt sensing her blatant staring, and she buried her face in her tumbler.

"I believe we have a...what's the word?" Patrick asked Gabe.

"Bridezilla," he supplied.

"Right. I believe we have one of those on our hands."

"She wants pink swans," Max interjected. "We have an idiot on our hands."

"You've got to be kidding,' she sputtered, looking to Gabe and Patrick who could only nod and drown their sorrows. "Swans don't come in pink."

"She read that a Saudi Arabian prince had pink swans at his wedding," Gabe said.

"Where do you find them?" she asked. "I mean, if she's ready to pay for—"

"You don't *find* them," Max said, crossing his boots on the table. "You *make* them."

Patrick leaned over and added more whiskey to his glass. She fought the urge to gulp down the rest of hers and shove her tumbler out for a refill. "You have to dip swans in red dye," he said.

"By hand." Max shook his head. "And guess who's job that would be." He jabbed his thumb at his own chest. "Mine."

She reveled in the warmth of the fire, the drink, the masculine camaraderie. She liked men. And, she really liked these men, Gabe occasionally included.

"Poor Max," she said and patted her former brother-in-law's shoulders.

"We're not doing it," Gabe said, rolling his head as if his neck was stiff. "It can't be good for the swans and I'm not endangering wildlife for the Fish-Stick Princess."

"Maybe you could talk to her," Patrick said, gesturing to her with his tumbler.

"Me?" Alice asked. "Why?"

"Talk reason to her, woman-to-woman." Patrick nodded as if he was on to something. "Your wedding was the loveliest thing I ever saw and so—"

"She's handling the kitchen, Dad," Gabe cut in, but it was too late. It was as if the memory of that flawless September day had plunked itself down on the table amongst them. Her mother's wedding dress. Her father's tears as he handed her to Gabe. Gabe's vows that he'd written himself. Max's speech that had them all laughing so hard they cried.

The kiss in front of all their friends and family that had felt like a promise. The small bulge of her belly where a new life kicked. A new start. The beginning of all things good and right and wonderful in her life.

She drained her glass and held it out for more.

Patrick dutifully refilled it. "Now," he said, "my wedding to your mother, that was a day for the books."

The room went still. Silent. Like a cathedral or, more appropriately, a tomb.

Gabe turned to stare at his father, his face hard and uncompromising. Carved from ice.

Alice held her breath to see how this particular bomb would detonate. No one ever mentioned Iris. Ever. The few times Alice had tried she'd been shut down so hard and so fast that she slept on the couch to prevent getting frostbite by sleeping next to Gabe.

She'd thought curiosity or concern for these men, alone for too long, had been frozen out of her by her marriage to Gabe. But sitting here now, the familiar refrain billowed in her like white smoke from a wet fire.

Poor guys.

"I'm going to get some work done," Gabe said. He stood, rubbing his free hand over his face and through his hair.

He looked tired. Worn. And she knew he took great pains to never look that way. Keeping the facade in place was paramount to Gabe.

"Maybe you should take a break," she said before she thought better of her concern. "Just relax. You won't do your inn any good if you get sick."

"The girl's got an idea," Patrick said and took a sip.

"You worry about you," Gabe said, throwing her words back in her face. "I'll worry about my inn."

She held up her hands, somehow knowing it would come to this, any effort to reach out on her part would be snubbed.

Gabe stared hard at his father for a minute, which Patrick pretended to ignore, and then he walked away, disappearing into the shadows outside the cheerful light of the fire.

Max snorted into the silence.

"What's wrong?" Alice asked, the temperature in the room still arctic despite the blaze in the oversize fireplace.

"Dad can't leave well enough alone," Max said, and then he stood up and left. Disappearing in the opposite direction from where Gabe had vanished.

Alice finally turned to Patrick, who sat with his head resting on the curved back of the sofa, his hand over the breast pocket of his shirt.

"What's going on here?" Alice asked.

She poured herself more whiskey, since the first two fingerfuls only made the demons silent, it didn't put them away. They were there, breathing and waiting.

"Nothing new."

Alice waited for some elaboration, but of course, true to Mitchell form, none came.

"Do you want to talk about it?" she asked.

He rolled his head sideways, his merry eyes were subdued, dark. "It's about their mother," he finally said.

Alice blinked and leaned back, stunned to her core. "The root?" she asked, using her pet name for Gabe's absentee mother.

"*The root?*"

"The root of all evil," she said. "The root of all Gabe's intimacy issues, his blind need for a family, his fear of—"

Patrick didn't even say good-night, he just stood, poured another inch of whiskey in his glass and walked into the shadows.

Alice sat there, slack jawed.

Thirty years ago, the woman had left all three men high and dry. Alice couldn't believe Patrick would be offended by her words, though clearly he was.

I should apologize, she thought and drained the last of her whiskey. *He's a good man, been nothing but kind to me despite the divorce. I need allies in this place and Patrick has always been a good ally.*

"Patrick, I'm sorry," she said, but only the creak of the stairs as he climbed them answered her.

The firelight played over the amber liquid in the bottle, the reflection cast waves of light across the floor. The fire was warm, the room empty, there was another four ounces in the bottle...

This was supposed to be a fresh start. She'd planned to wake up early tomorrow, prove to Gabe that she took this seriously. That she was the same old Alice, perfectionist and workaholic.

She was excited about all of that.

"One more drink," she sighed. Alice grabbed the bottle, stretched out her feet and settled in.

The next morning Gabe stood in an empty cold kitchen and felt the past wash over him. When would he learn? He shook his head and put his hand on the cold coffeepot. Expecting more from the women in his life had only led to this moment. This...disappointment.

First his mom and now Alice.

Again.

He should have known by the way she watched the bottle of whiskey last night, her eyes gleaming like a starving dog, chained just out of reach of food.

She'd gotten drunk. She'd gotten drunk and now it was 9:00 a.m., well past the time any chef would be up and working, considering the amount of prep she had to do. Instead she would be hungover and it was only the second day.

Grabbing the keys from the hook he hung them on, he hit the door hard and left the inn.

He tried to be reasonable, to understand her position, how awkward it must be for her to come here surrounded by the Mitchell men. He tried. But failed.

I'm such an idiot! he thought, slamming the door on his old BMW. *I should have listened to my gut and walked away from her when I saw her drinking at her house.* He yanked the wheel and spun out of the parking area, spitting gravel and pulling up grass.

She's too damaged. Too locked in the past. No wonder she lost

Zinnia. No wonder we could never work it out, the woman is so absorbed in her own pain she can never see what she's doing to other people.

Like him.

She never saw what she did to him. She hadn't when she was screaming at him during their marriage, and she didn't now. He needed her and she didn't care.

She's gone, he decided, speeding down the turnpike toward Daphne. *When I get back I'll tell her to pack up and hit the road. I can't take this. I don't have to. I'll figure something else out.*

Gabe rolled down the window, hoping the cool morning air would chill him out a little. It didn't work. Resolving to fire her didn't work. Alice, when he was mad at her, lived in his brain and under his skin.

This was his fault. Totally his fault.

To even think of bringing her here had been asking for this.

He pulled a hand through his hair and tried to force her out of his head. He was going on a date after all, no matter how unorthodox. Meeting Daphne with Alice stuck in his head wasn't fair to Daphne or him.

He wondered briefly if it was fair to Alice to fire her when she so clearly needed help. He pushed that thought away. He'd spent too many years trying to help her.

He was done saving Alice from herself.

He turned up the radio, found "Baba O'Reiley" and sang along with The Who tune. He'd managed to push Alice out of his head once, he could do it again.

Starting now.

Twenty minutes later, with her only running circles in the back of his brain, he pulled up in front of the pretty, white-and-yellow farmhouse and climbed out of his car. A black-and-brown dog charged him, but Daphne, standing in the doorway, called the beast off.

"Hi, Gabe," she said, her smile sweet and girlish in a way that called up masculine things in himself. He wanted to hug her.

"Daphne," he said with a grin.

"Come on in, I've got a pot on." She led the way into her kitchen. His mood recovered, spreading a warm glow around him. Her house was perfect, looking messy and well lived in. The pine floors were worn smooth, the curtains in the window faded by the sun, boots and shoes piled up at the door.

It was exactly what he wanted for his inn. Someday he wanted his great-grandkids leading their respective lovers and friends through the front door that he'd built with his brother and dad.

Just thinking about it gave him chills.

"My meeting with your chef went very well yesterday," Daphne said, looking at him over her shoulder.

There went his good mood, his warm glow dimmed. He couldn't even go on a date to get away from her.

"I gave her some herb samples, all of the lettuce and basil she ordered and the purple potatoes, broccoli and carrots." Daphne pulled two mugs from the whitewashed cupboard, and grabbed the coffee carafe and set it all on the table.

Her smile was effervescent, huge, bright and warm enough to heat cold rooms. Not at all like Alice's, which seemed broken. Sick.

Stop it! he ordered himself. *Stop thinking about her. There are no comparisons between Alice and Daphne.*

"Cream?" Daphne asked, heading for the fridge.

"No, thanks," he said and she stopped and sat down at the table.

"Me, neither." She glanced at him sideways with a look that seemed young and flirtatious, despite the slight gray in her blond hair, and the wrinkles around her eyes.

Wrinkles and gray hair that he liked, considering he had some of it himself.

"Gets in the way of the caffeine," he said, taking a sip of the brew she'd poured.

"Exactly."

She sat back and suddenly the silence seemed to have an awkward weight and heft. *I don't have time for this*, he thought again, suddenly anxious to get going. *I have those press releases to send out and the Web site to update. I have to fire Alice and find—*

"We're supposed to be relaxing," Daphne said, brushing her braid over her shoulder. "And I think both of us are making lists."

He nodded. "Guilty. The curse of owning your own business."

"The plus side is we can make up for whatever work we're not doing right now later. So—" she took a deep breath "—let's stop making lists and act like normal people."

"Normal people..." He narrowed his eyes. "I can't quite remember how they act."

She laughed, the sound husky and deep, and it made him smile. He did have time for this, because if he didn't make time to date, to meet nice women over coffee, he'd end up like his dad and brother. He'd end up living with them forever.

"Your chef, Alice? She's an intense woman," Daphne said. "Striking. She seems very sad."

Well, talking about his ex-wife wasn't really what he had in mind.

"She's complicated," he said and took a sip of coffee. Telling Daphne that Alice was his ex-wife seemed a bit precipitous since she wouldn't be around much longer.

"Hey, Mom—" A miniature version of Daphne— complete with the long white-blond braid and bright green galoshes—came running up the stairs from the basement.

"Hey, Helen." Daphne opened her arm and the young girl hugged her mother's side. "What's up?"

"Matt's coming over. His mom has to go to the store."

"Okay. You guys can help me in the greenhouse."

Helen turned up her nose and Daphne kissed it. "You might have a day off kindergarten, but I still have to work," she said. "You two help me out in the greenhouse and I'll take you for ice cream in town."

Helen nodded, the deal struck, then ran back downstairs.

Gabe felt his heart expand, fill like a balloon until it threatened to lift him off his chair.

Family. His pulse seemed to chant it for him.

"My daughter," Daphne said needlessly. "Her father and I divorced about three years ago."

Gabe nodded and looked around, noticing the things he'd missed before. The drawings on the fridge. The kids' cereal on the counter. The Barbie book bag set up by the door.

A family. Right here.

He looked at Daphne with new eyes. His heart so full in his chest he could barely breathe.

"Do you like kids?" she asked.

Gabe nodded. "Yes," he said. "I've always wanted kids."

The headache from her too-short night and too much whiskey had been muted to a dull throb. The coffee helped. The cooking helped more. Alice's kitchen was warm—a chicken, three lemons, a bay leaf, onion, carrots and celery boiled away in a huge pot on the stove, creating stock she would freeze for later use. The crisp sweet smell of mint wafted from her food processor as she added a little more sugar to her mint and walnut pesto.

The dairy farm she'd visited at dawn had already delivered the cream and milk and some of the owner's early attempts at cheese. The ricotta was good. Not great, but okay.

She took another sip of coffee, and tried to encourage that small fire of happiness that was back in her belly. If she could just stay in this kitchen all day and never talk to Gabe or—

"Pack your bags."

She whirled to find him in the doorway, angry and bristling as if he'd heard her thoughts.

"I want you gone," he said.

7

I f Alice was surprised, she hid it well. Her face was empty, composed. Her eyebrows slightly arched as if to say "excuse me?" The cup of coffee in her hand steady.

"I'm not kidding," Gabe said as coldly as possible. He bit his tongue against what he really wanted to say: *I need to be free of you. I can't get on with my life with you here.* "I want you out."

"Why?" she finally asked, setting down her cup as though it might break in her hand. "What's happened?"

"It doesn't matter. This isn't going to work."

"I think I deserve an explanation," she said. Her anger fueled his, especially since she didn't have any right to hers.

"What time did you finally get out of bed today?" he asked. She opened her mouth but he didn't want to hear what she had to say. He knew the truth. He'd always known it and he was a fool to try to convince himself this situation could go a different way. "How late did you stay up drinking last night? It was Monday for crying out loud. Your first day and you decide to get drunk?"

"Gabe—"

He shook his head, feeling oddly emotional. As if a great boulder of pain and anger was bearing down on him. "I was an idiot to think this was going to work."

"I don't understand what's going on here." The white flesh of her neck flushed slightly pink and he nearly relished that small sign of her involvement. Her caring. Her goddamn interest in what was happening. "You're firing me?"

"Yes."

"Why?"

Because you're a drunk. You're unstable. "Because this is my home," he said instead, surprising himself with the honesty. His body was hot and he couldn't control it, couldn't calm himself. His throat hurt from not yelling. "Mine. I made it. You can't have this one. You can't take this one from me. Or ruin it."

They both blinked while his words rocked the very foundation of the building.

"You think that's what I want to do?" she asked, so composed, except for her hands, which trembled before she pressed them against her apron. Her lips were white.

"I don't think you want to, but you will."

She looked away for a moment, blinking, and he wondered if he'd gone too far. Compassion for this woman he used to love with an all-consuming force welled up in him, slow like black tar.

But he refused to give in to it. The Riverview, his sanity, his home—it was all at stake now.

Alice didn't know why she didn't open her mouth and tell him the truth. Why she, in fact, didn't scream the truth from the rooftops and rub his face in his wrong conclusions and allegations.

Because he's right. Part of her agreed with him.

I am a failure. Everything I touch turns to mud.

She brushed her hands of mint and turned to leave. She'd have her bags packed and be back in Albany with a glass of wine before the real pain set in.

"We went to the dairy farm outside of Coxsackie," Max said from the door to the dining room, where he'd been standing for God knows how long. The blush and emotion she'd been able to barely control flooded her and she put her hand on the chopping block for balance because her head felt light. Her body too awkward. "She wanted to go early to see the first milking."

"Max," she started to stay, ready to tell him she didn't need defending.

"You were going to let him think the worst," he said, not looking at her.

He sauntered to the coffeepot and smirked at Gabe, practically egging him into a fight. Max loved to catch Gabe flat-footed and from her ex-husband's openmouthed, slack-jawed look of surprise, she had to guess Max won this round.

She'd been defended. The truth was out and all it took was one look at Gabe's face to realize it didn't matter.

He wanted her gone, drunk or not, working or not.

Gabe shut his mouth, shook his head and seemed to gather himself. She could read him like a book. He still didn't want her here, but now he had no reason to fire her.

She fumbled with the ties on her apron.

He was right—this was a mistake. For both of them. If this failed, if she screwed this up...it would hurt. More than what she felt right now. If she cared more...if she worked longer with these beautiful foods, in this beautiful room and then had to leave...the pain would magnify. Double and triple over.

Max poured himself a coffee. "Stop being an ass," he told his brother and slapped Gabe on the back before heading outside. Alice wished fervently she could join him.

"Why didn't you say something?" Gabe asked.

"I thought I was supposed to be running the kitchen. You weren't going to interfere," she managed to say, when what she wanted to say was, "You're right. What's the point of defending myself against the truth."

"But I accused you—"

"Of what? Drinking too much?" She shrugged. "I did. I do."

He licked his lips, his gaze so steady, so rock solid that she ached from the pressure. Nothing about her was rock solid. Nothing was steady. She was a house of cards and there was a fire beneath her.

"But you could have told me what your plans were. I don't think it's—"

She let out some of the steam building in her, vented it on him. "Considering—" her voice dripped with sarcasm "—your date this morning with the young mother, I didn't want to bother you with details like milk."

He rocked back on his heels. "Young mother?" His incredulous laughter felt like acid against her skin and heart. "You have got to get over this. It all happened years ago."

It's right now, she wanted to howl. *It's every minute I'm not a mother.*

They both took deep breaths until the tension in the air dissipated, something they'd learned to do the hard way in the last few months they were together.

"This isn't about Daphne," Gabe said, his voice soft. "And it's not about our marriage."

"And it's not about me drinking. So what is it, Gabe? What do you really need from me right now that I'm not giving you?"

"I need a commitment," he said plainly. "You're my chef, you're a cornerstone for my business, and you've got me so nervous right now that I'm ready to do it myself."

"Tomato soup from a can and grilled-cheese sandwiches? The bride will love that." She mocked him, mocked the meal he used to make for her that once brought her such joy.

He winced, then rubbed his hands through his hair, putting the blond waves on end. The mask he wore—the I-can-do-it-all Gabe Mitchell mask—fell away for just a moment and she could see him. The real him—small and nervous and sleepless inside the suit of professionalism he wore—behind the smoke and mirrors.

The great and powerful Oz was at the end of his rope.

She trembled on the edge of something, on the edge of her solitary existence, on the edge of her combined failures that she wore like armor to prevent herself from risking too much again.

She tried to remember how she'd once been, when she'd taken risks, when she'd loved her life and her work, when collabo-rating with Gabe had been as exhilarating as making love to him.

Give a little, Alice. Give a tiny bit. Offer something that he doesn't have to fight for.

"Look, I can handle prep and cook for your guests. But I need some help for that wedding by the end of this month." Her voice was gruff, her compromise hidden and buried beneath her begrudging tone.

Gabe blinked, then blinked again. "I can find you help before then. I've got feelers—"

"I'm telling you, you don't need to. I can handle it—just not the wedding."

"That's a lot of work," he said. "I'm expecting twenty guests in May and I'm still taking reservations."

She shot him a *puh-leeze* look. She'd handled more than that as a sous chef with laryngitis and a broken oven.

"All that work? Really?" he asked.

She nodded. "It's not like there is anything else to do," she said. And work would keep her mind off other things. Like booze. Like Zinnia. Like failed marriages and her ex-husband dating.

"Okay," Gabe said. "I can hire—"

"I'll hire someone," she interrupted, "from my salary for a larger percentage of ownership." The words toppled out of her mouth willy-nilly and awkward. She had very little experience with compromise.

She managed a quick look at Gabe to see if his response was favorable.

"Oh, shut your mouth," she said, exasperated by his shocked expression. "Let's both be reasonable."

"Those are great terms," he said and stuck out his hand.

She slid her hand into his giant paw and quickly tried to remove it, but he gripped her, his thick callused fingers closing in around hers.

"Al." Her nickname again and the room shrank, the space between them was too small. She could feel his heat and his breath against her face. "Please stop drinking."

She shook her head. She should and she would. But it wouldn't be because of he'd told her to do it. "No. What I do on my time is my business."

"I can't—"

"I've committed, Gabe." She finally looked right into his eyes, the brilliant blue that could burn her or freeze her, that could bring her to life or shut her down in a hundred different ways. Belatedly she realized what she'd done. She'd tied her fortune to a man who could destroy her —again.

"You won't get any more from me," she told him and somehow they both understood that it wasn't only work they talked about. His hand was hot in hers. The callus on his thumb seemed suddenly personal, the proof of his labor too much for her to witness.

"Alice, about Daphne—"

She jerked her hand away.

"I have a lot of work to do." She turned from him, retying the strings of her apron.

"Me, too," he murmured. She heard him go into his office and shut the door.

The breath she hadn't realized she'd been holding leaked out of her, and she nearly sagged.

A business card appeared under her nose and, startled, she jerked upright. Max, the damn sneak stood there, his expression unreadable. "Sheriff in town runs an AA meeting out of the station on Sunday nights," he said.

"I'm not an alcoholic," she said.

He shrugged. "Not really my business," he said, "but if you want to talk to him tell him I gave you his number."

"Max." She tried to laugh. "I don't need the card."

But he just stood there, so different from Gabe yet at the core of both of them lay the same stubborn compassion that ran them both ragged in different ways.

Once upon a time Max had wanted to save the world and all Gabe had wanted was to save was his own family.

She sighed and took the card knowing Max would stand there all day if she didn't.

A week later, Alice checked her watch and decided an afternoon coffee break was in order.

Coffee, she decided, *some fresh air and I'll think about those potatoes that need to be dealt with.*

The sun sat in the crook of the western mountains and the property was a dramatically different world than the one she'd greeted at dawn this morning. The fog had burned off, the cacophony of springtime insects that had seemed so loud this morning were gone, replaced by the sound of Max and his gang of street thugs clearing brush.

A week after her compromise with Gabe and she was seriously regretting her decision to do all the prep herself. Not that she'd ever admit that to Gabe, who'd been staying out of her way, even as he watched her like a hawk, waiting, she was sure, for her to screw up.

So she worked and pretended he wasn't there, though she felt him at her back so much that when she slept she could feel him there, curled against her the way he had when they were married.

She woke up every morning, turned on and annoyed. And it only got worse throughout the day.

But all of this watching and ignoring had to come to an end. She had a menu coming together that she needed to be sampled and she didn't have any details on the wedding. Numbers. Themes. Money.

Sooner or later they were actually going to have to work

together. But until then it was best they avoided talking to each other. He called up things in her that she hated, emotions that were ugly and petty.

In the meantime, she was up to her sore elbows in work. She'd forgotten how hard it was building a kitchen from scratch. There were deliveries to put away: heavy bags of onions and potatoes from Athens Organics; sides of beef that she preferred to butcher herself, which was no easy task.

And then there was the constant boiling, baking, basting and freezing of stocks, marinades and flavored oils. She fell into bed at the end of every day too tired to even think of drinking and woke up every morning sore to the bottom of her feet but her mind already working on the day's chores.

Today it was potatoes. Gnocchi and latke. The huge bag of potatoes sat in the pantry mocking her and her tired biceps.

She wished she had some help, just a little, for the afternoon. But she'd made this bed, she would lie in it. After her break.

She slid on her sunglasses and sat down on the small hill behind the kitchen, flanking the makeshift parking lot, and watched Max herd the kids like they were cattle. Or cats.

"Hey," he said, his voice echoing through the woods as he emerged from the tree line. "Stop slacking, this is our last tree."

He and a girl dragged the shorn trunk of a fallen poplar toward the huge pile of debris they'd gathered in a cleared area next to the lodge.

"We gonna burn this stuff or what?" Cameron appeared from the woods, half-heartedly pulling a limb from the tree behind him. "Because I think that would only be the right way to end this whole thing, you know?"

"No," Max said succinctly, rolling the thick trunk under some of the brush at the base of the pile. "I don't."

Alice couldn't tell if Max and the kids were a match made in hell or heaven. From the closed-down, locked-up expression on Max's face she bet he wasn't sure, either.

"This huge tree goes down, no one knows. It sits there in the woods, rotting, bugs eating it, animals pooping on it. That's no way for a tree to go," Cameron said and Alice found herself warming up to the kid with his overworked sense of drama. "We gotta burn it. Put it out of its misery."

"Be quiet," Max said and Cameron, after a few more jokes on the tree's behalf, did. Alice was a little surprised at the progress Max had made with the mouthy kid. He wore a hat that kept the hair out of his eyes, and his pants, still too big, were held up by a belt. And he was working.

Maybe now that he was house-trained she could actually work with him in the kitchen. He could run his mouth and peel potatoes at the same time.

"We're not done," Max said, heading back to the forest, and a chorus of groans followed him even though the kids didn't. "Let's go," he said. "Anything you're doing right now is better than what you'd be doing in juvie."

That shut up some of them, Cameron included, and they started after Max.

"Max," she called, pushing herself to her feet. "Can I borrow Cameron for the day?" she asked.

Max looked at her, then at Cameron, who made a face as though she'd asked him to run around naked, and finally shrugged. "If you want him."

"Hey! You can't just trade me whenever you feel like it!" Cameron cried.

"It's easier than what you're doing," she said.

"I'm there," Cameron said quickly, and stepped out of line to head her way.

"Good luck," Max called over his shoulder. "If he gives you trouble, send him out to me."

"Will do," she yelled back.

Cameron came to stand in front of her, his face scratched and dirty and his eyes on his shoes.

"You gonna give me trouble?" she asked and he shrugged.

I can't ask for more honesty than that.

"Well," she said, as she led him inside. "It's time for you to meet your new best friend—a potato peeler."

He groaned, but he followed.

Gabe closed his e-mail and sat back with a grin. Four more guests thanks to his Internet promotion, plus Bridezilla had capitulated on the swans—thank God—and had promised him final guest-list numbers by the beginning of next week. Though he wouldn't hold his breath for that, so far the guest list had swelled and receded at least five times.

She'd decided on a band rather than the quartet, and the singer had e-mailed him their requirements, which weren't too bad.

With blue marker in hand he turned to update his wall-size calendar.

Someone knocked at his office door. It could only be Alice since his father and brother didn't believe in things such as closed doors and polite knocks.

"Come on in," he said. They'd been walking careful circles around each other for the past week and a half—smiling politely and staying out of each other's way. But he'd been watching her and if she was drinking, it didn't show. The woman was a chef possessed. And he couldn't be more relieved.

"Gabe," she said from the doorway, her voice cool and stark, letting him know she was here for business. He nearly rolled his eyes. Alice always wore her intentions on her sleeve and the tone of her voice let everyone know what her next move was.

She thought she was going to put his feet to the fire right now. As a partner and chef she thought she had that right.

And, he considered, she probably did.

He grunted while writing in the Andersons and Pursators on the third weekend in August. They would share the five-bedroom cabin closest to the lodge.

"Earth to Gabe," she said, annoyed, and he finally turned, capping his pen.

He shook his head with a laugh. "Sorry. A lot's going on."

"Right, well, me, too." Her tone was all business and he didn't want to fight. Not anymore. They needed to work together. He just needed to figure out how to get them from here to there in as little amount of time as possible. "I wanted to talk about a few things with you," she said, still in the doorway.

Sunlight streamed in behind her and lit the black hair escaping the bun she always wore while she worked, turning the runaway strands red.

In the week and a half she'd been here she'd managed to get some color on her face, her lips were pink, and she'd lost some of the fragile tragic look she'd had when he'd first seen her behind Johnny O's.

"You look good," he said, putting her off stride, which had been his intention. "Healthy."

Her fingers darted to her hair and she turned her face to the side for the shortest second, a small uncontrolled moment of self-consciousness. The gesture pinged through him, turning his compliment into a double-edged sword that sliced though his gut.

"Thanks," she finally said.

He nodded and looked away, his throat dry. But the tension around her was eradicated. Compliments were the best way to disarm a person, always worked. "What did you need?" he asked.

"Information about this wedding. I've got some sample menus, but I don't know anything about the event."

"I have a conference call with them at the beginning of next week." He glanced at the calendar behind him and quickly wrote the time of the call into his busy work week. "I'm supposed to get final numbers and details then. Why don't you join me."

"On the call?" she asked, clearly surprised.

"Sure." He shrugged. She'd compromised with him, the least he could do was try to make her job easier. His life got much easier by having her deal directly with Bridezilla and her flesh-eating mother rather than through him.

Brilliant, really, why didn't I think of this earlier?

"It'll be easier for everyone," he said. "I'm probably going to need some of your ideas on decorations—"

She smiled.

"Are you laughing at me?" he asked, knowing she was. This moment of ease, of light conversation was too nice to give up.

"You're great with leather and black-and-white photography," she said, summing up the decor of every apartment and restaurant he'd ever owned. "I would imagine wedding receptions will be a bit beyond you."

"You have better ideas?"

"About a million," she said, her dark eyes gleaming.

God, she's pretty when she's happy.

And it had been so long since he'd seen her happy.

The skin along his arms and chest twitched with the sudden urge to hold her.

"See—" he got swept up in their sudden chemistry "—I knew you were the right person to bring in on this."

That might have gone too far. His silver tongue had led him astray and what he'd said was too close to a lie. They both knew he didn't choose to bring her, they'd both been too desperate for anything else. The color faded slightly from her face.

"I'm happy to help out," she said and the air between them changed again, turned cold. Her lush mouth compressed to a thin line.

"Thank you, Alice. The call is on Monday, late afternoon."

A huge crash from the kitchen made her whirl in the doorway and he braced himself for some minor emergency. Some five-hundred-dollar stand-up mixer perhaps, or another two-hundred-dollar hospital visit for his brother who tended to get overconfident around saws.

"Cameron?" Alice cried. "You all right?"

"Fine," the disembodied voice of the kid Gabe barely remembered yelled back, clearly disgusted.

"Cameron?" he asked. "You changed your mind about having the kid help out?" He was surprised on a number of fronts. The kid had enough attitude to light up New York

State, and Alice, since the last miscarriage and the failed in vitro procedures, had gone way out of her way to avoid children of all ages.

Maybe she's healing, he thought, his stomach twisting with hope and sadness, a chronic sensation left over from his marriage. *Maybe she's finally letting go.*

"Just for today," she said. She turned back toward him, her lips fighting a smile. "He knocked over the bucket of potato peels. He's covered head to foot."

He laughed. "Beats hauling wood with Max."

"That's what I told him."

"So, when do you want to dazzle me with your menus?"

"Well, with Cameron taking some of the load off today, I think I could pull it together for tomorrow night, Friday. I know we discussed things already, but I had to tweak the duck and so far I haven't found any good—"

"I trust you, Alice," he said, shocking both of them. "You don't have to defend your decisions. Max, Dad and I will be ready to be dazzled tomorrow night."

She eyed him suspiciously. "This is not the Gabe Mitchell I know. The Gabe Mitchell who likes—"

"Gabe Mitchell is busy," he said. "He's busy and tired and he knows, very well, how good you are."

Another compliment. Wasn't he full of them today? This one had slipped out unbidden. Caught him unprepared. The truth was, he had intended to ride her the entire time she was here. Since her latest compromise, however, she'd been on point and he could rest easy. It was a gift, almost, one he wasn't sure didn't tick, about to blow up in his face.

"Thanks,' she said. "Again."

"I, ah...need to get to work."

"Right." She pushed herself off the doorway. "Gabe, what I said last week, about Daphne—"

"Don't worry," he said quickly, heat scorching his neck. This was the apology he'd thought he wanted, but now he'd rather continue with this comfortable unsaid truce between them. He didn't want to discuss his love life with his ex-wife, not when things were going so well. "It's forgotten."

"I was out of line," she said, pressing on, as she always did when he wanted her to stop. "It's none of my business and she's a lovely woman."

"Yes, she is. Thanks for the apology." He hoped she'd leave it at that, that she wouldn't ruin this fragile equilibrium.

He glanced at her, lit by sun, her chef whites unbuttoned, revealing a green shirt underneath. She smiled, awkward and sad, a different version of the bristly woman she'd become over the years with him.

She looked like the twenty-four-year-old he'd met ten years ago. Sweet and smart with the devil in her eyes and the corner of her mouth.

And his whole body, all of it, reacted, leaned toward her with the old desire.

He didn't need this. He didn't need a reminder of the good times, of the woman he'd loved rather than the woman he'd grown to hate.

She was beautiful, she was an asset, and she couldn't leave soon enough.

8

The envelope Patrick had just signed for burned in his hand. He wondered if he would be branded, his palm black with the words *to my husband*.

It had been three weeks since the first letter and a week and half since he'd mailed his response, via the lawyer. A week and half of checking the horizon for the black sedan bringing another letter from her. A week and half of eating better food that tasted like dirt and sat like stones in his stomach. A week and a half of wondering if he could ever change his sons' minds.

"Who was that?" Max asked, arriving silently from nowhere, to suddenly be at his side. Patrick watched the car brake at the end of the gravel road, then turn left toward the two-lane highway that would take it to the interstate.

"No one," Patrick said, shoving the envelope into his back pocket. "Letter from my lawyer."

"Everything okay?" Max asked and Patrick could feel his son's police officer gaze searching him for clues.

"Fine, just some information about investments."

"My inheritance?" Max asked and took a slug from the bottle of water he held.

"Sure," he said, distracted. "I better get back to work. I'm finishing electrical on the gazebo today so the Fish-Stick Princess can have her pink twinkle lights."

Max lifted his plastic bottle in farewell and headed off for the forest and his trail blazing.

Patrick nearly ran to the gazebo, the warm wind at his back pushing him toward the freshly built structure with the view of the Catskills and the Hudson.

He stood on the concrete slab he'd poured and leveled himself and ripped open the envelope.

You're not giving me the truth, Pat. I could always tell. Does Gabe still take after you, so eager to smooth away the bad stuff?

When you say the boys are coming around to the idea, does that mean they are actually allowing you to talk about me? Or does Max simply walk away? You always were a silver-tongued man, Pat. But I can tell from what you're not saying that my boys don't want to see me.

Patrick raked his upper lip with his teeth, guilt over the decision he'd made years ago forcing its way through the righteous anger and all his good intentions.

I didn't argue with you, Pat, when you told me to stay away. Both times. And I couldn't blame you. I know what I was and it's why I left. I believed you and the boys were better without me, without my problems. But I sent you the signed divorce papers and you never signed them. Why isn't this marriage over, Pat? If you hate me so much? Why aren't we free of each other?

He nearly laughed. As if a piece of paper could make them free. God had joined them. Walking away or signing legal documents had nothing to do with it.

I've done what you asked. Twice. It's broken my heart a thousand times a day, but I agreed with you. I left, I forfeited any rights I might have claimed. You were their father, raising them in my place. I bowed to your wishes and I have not been in touch with any of you for over twenty-five years.

But things are changed now, Pat. Things are different. I need to see you. I need to see my sons.

It won't be for long and they don't even need to know who I am. Please, Pat. My husband. I want to come home to you.

His knees buckled and he sat on the wooden railing. He lifted his face to the wind; the smell of the river and pine blew up from the valley, but it did not dry his tears.

Iris was coming home.

Alice scratched her nose on the sleeve of her chef jacket since her hands were covered in slime and chicken meat from the carcass she was tearing apart. The broth was already cooling in the fridge, to be put to use tomorrow night for the menu rollout. This meat would be put to use in the Thai stir-fry she craved for dinner. The clock above the stove told her she had about two hours before she needed to get that stir-fry cooking.

The door at her elbow swung open and she whirled, startled, splattering Patrick with chicken juice.

"Oh, no, Patrick." She grabbed the dish towel that was tucked into the waist of her apron and handed it to him by the smallest corner she could. "I'm so sorry."

"Don't worry." He smiled, then wiped at his flannel shirt and, oddly, his eyes. "I should know better than to sneak up on a woman murdering a chicken."

She laughed and picked up the leg she'd stripped meat from. "It's for a good cause, I promise."

"Have you seen either of my boys, preferably Gabe?"

"Not for hours, sorry." She noticed, as he seemed to take great efforts not to look directly at her, that his eyes were red. If he were any other person and not a Mitchell man, she'd think he had been weeping.

"Patrick." She dropped the chicken and wiped her own hands. "Are you okay?"

"You bet." Patrick's smile was wide and, to the uninitiated, believable. But she'd spent years with this man's offspring, translating the many smiles to mean any number of things, and this smile tried just a shade too hard.

She knew better than to call him on it, however, so, as she had in her marriage, she approached the topic sideways.

"I'm glad you stopped in," she said. "I am so sorry about the first night I was here. I should not have said anything about Iris and my apology was almost as hideous as what I said. I've felt bad about it for two weeks, but I just haven't had a chance to find you and say something."

The smile twitched and she knew that whatever was making this man's eyes red had something to do with Iris.

"I was a little out of sorts," she continued. "Being back with—"

"Would Gabe and Max have been better off with their mother?" Patrick asked suddenly and Alice was rocked back on her heels. "I mean, not instead of me, but if she had been in the picture, would my boys have benefited?"

"Of course," she said cautiously after a moment. "I mean, only if she wanted to be there. If she was there and didn't want to be, well, then they were certainly better off with just a father who adored them."

"Really?" he asked, white and stricken, and Alice felt trapped. "If she had wanted to come back—"

"But she didn't come back," she raced to say. "She left and no one heard from her again."

Patrick went white and stared at his hands, at his thumb as it worried a cut on his palm.

Alice didn't know what to think with this uncharacteristically insecure man in front of her.

She should say something, do something, to bring the regular Patrick back, but she didn't have that power. His vulnerability called out to her and she could only stand there and bleed silent sympathy.

"She left, walked away without a word. Like none of us mattered," he said. "What was I supposed to do?"

"Exactly what you did," she said, tense and uncomfortable. There were a lot of things wrong with her ex-husband that could no doubt be traced back to being raised by a single father—by this single father who spent so much time pretending everything was fine—without the influence of a mother, but she could hardly say that to Patrick now.

He nodded slowly. "Right," he said, his nod gaining speed and, as though he'd never left, the assured Patrick was back pink cheeked and smiling. "You're right, sweetie." He gave her a loud smacking kiss on the cheek. "Don't worry about the other night," he said. "We were all a little out of sorts. We'll try it again tonight, without the arguments."

She knew, of course, what he was referring to. They'd sit

in front of the fire and share a drink, but she couldn't do that. She'd committed. Like it or not. She'd stocked the kitchen, built a menu, worked herself to the bone from dawn until dusk without killing her ex-husband or taking a drink.

All good things.

"I'm sorry, Patrick." She winced. "I am going to be so busy the next few weeks. Tomorrow night I'm rolling out my menu and on Monday I've got my first call with Bridezilla."

"Too bad. Don't let my son run you ragged."

"Not likely," she quipped because she knew he'd like it and, as she'd expected, he laughed on his way out the door. The kitchen fell silent as if he'd never been there.

Wary of the lingering chicken grease, she wiped a stray black curl from her forehead with her wrist and went back to work. What had brought on Patrick's mood? Hopefully it was over and they could all not talk about things such as regrets and what-ifs and second chances.

The next morning Alice woke up, her hands sore, her lower back in knots, and realized she needed about a million cloves of garlic peeled—on top of putting together the menu—and Cameron was just the man for the job. He'd gotten through the potatoes and the carrots yesterday.

"You sure?" Max asked while they both glared at the coffee machine, waiting for it to finish hissing and puffing. "He's working out?"

"Well, he hasn't cut himself or me. And as long as I don't

actually listen to him talk all day it seems to work out." She shrugged. "I need the help and he's doing okay."

"Enough said." Max filled his travel coffee mug, even though the machine wasn't done, and Alice stuck her mug under the stream of coffee running onto the burner.

"I'll send him your way when he arrives," Max said and disappeared out the door.

"Send who where?" Gabe's rusty voice asked from the dining-room door. She turned only to find him, hair standing on end and blurry eyed, propped up against the door frame.

"You look like crap," she said and pulled out the mug she'd noticed was his favorite, despite the chip in the lip.

"Ah, is it any wonder we couldn't make it work?" he asked without any heat and she found herself smiling at this morning version of Gabe. He'd always looked like a little boy in the morning, someone in desperate need of coffee and a long cuddle.

She'd enjoyed being the one to cuddle him, kissing his forehead and warming her cold feet against his thighs until his brain fully clicked into gear.

"I had this dream last night that I was being chased by pink swans," he said, gratefully accepting the coffee she'd poured for him.

"Stress dreams, you need a break," she said.

He nodded and slurped from his mug.

"Did your dad find you yesterday?" she asked. "Just before dinner, he was looking for you."

"He found me." His voice changed. Cold Gabe stood before her, his blurry eyes gone, his easy morning repartee frozen out of him.

Is he okay? What did he want? What's going on with your

mother? Did you listen to him or freeze him out like you are me right now?

All of that and dozens of other questions burned at her lips, but she dammed them. The lessons of her marriage were ingrained and impossible to forget.

"Good," she said and turned to her notebook of lists. "Have a good day."

She was too tired, sore and preoccupied to do anything else.

∼

Cameron arrived sullen and filthy just after three.

"Good God," she cried. "What happened to you?"

"You and those potatoes," he shot back, tossing his greasy brown hair over his eyes.

"Well, didn't you shower last night? Or this morning?" She noticed he wore the same baggy black T-shirt with the anarchy symbol across the front. She doubted he even knew what it meant. She wondered what his home must be like if a kid could wander around covered in dirt for two days.

"It wouldn't matter if I was outside dragging trees around," he said.

"Well, you're not. You're in my kitchen. Let's get you cleaned up." She grabbed the bar of lava soap that had the power to remove the smell of garlic from hands and shoved him toward the employee bathrooms. "Lose the shirt and I'll find you something else to wear."

"I'm not wearing your clothes." He sneered at her tomato-red Henley that she had put on for dramatic flair underneath her chef whites.

She nearly laughed at herself now.

"I'll find you something," she promised and nudged him into the bathroom.

Ten minutes later he emerged, soaking wet and shirtless. He looked embarrassed standing in the doorway, his thin arms crossed over his concave chest, two inches of his underwear visible at the top of his ratty blue jeans.

Poor kid, she thought, nearly smiling. But she didn't because intuition told her that would just kill the fifteen-year-old. Instead she chucked her smallest, oldest chef jacket and pants at him.

He caught them and vanished, doing a strange side step into the bathroom before turning around. She just managed to see the purple-and-yellow bruise on his shoulder blade before the door slammed shut, the sound louder than her strangled gasp.

She knew most of the kids in Max's program were from troubled homes, but seeing the proof of it was shocking. Searing.

For a brief period of time after the divorce, she went to a support group called Mother's Without Babies. Everyone was on a different place on the spectrums of grief and anger and acceptance. But one thing they all shared was a profound horror, a gnawing sadness that there were parents in the world who would hurt their children. Children the women in that group would have died for.

And she felt the same primal rage, looking at the shut bathroom door, as she had sitting in that group, her grief still so raw she couldn't look at children on the street.

The door swung open and Cameron stood there, hair dripping, clothes a little too big, but surprisingly not too bad since he was tall for his age.

"What happened to your back?" she asked point-blank.

"Nothing."

"Your dad or—"

His face twisted in disdain. "Please," he scoffed.

"He didn't hit you?"

"Nah." Cameron shook his head. "I think I did it two days ago hauling wood."

She watched him, having years of experience with the excuses created by prep chefs and waitresses and dishwashers. She was pretty good at spotting a lie. And all her radars told her Cameron wasn't lying.

"No one hit you?"

He shook his head. "No one even notices me," he said. "Now, what disgusting thing am I supposed to do today."

She set him up at the chopping block with the cloves of garlic and explained how to deskin them.

"I'm gonna stink!" he protested.

"It's not as if you smell like roses right now."

"Who wants to smell like roses?"

"It's an expression." The small tiny curve in the corner of his mouth told her he was giving her a hard time and she had to fight herself from ruffling his hair.

"Get to work," she joked and set up her own station of chopping the garlic he peeled.

She had about two hours before she needed to get to work on the menu rollout. She'd already set the table in the dining room, putting a little effort into the flowers and candles, letting Gabe see how it should be done, rather than the tiny bud vases and two votives he usually used.

"So, like, how'd you become a cook?" Cameron asked.

"Chef," she corrected, just to give him a hard time.

"Right, whatever." He rolled his eyes at her and she couldn't remember the last time she'd had this much fun with her staff. Torturing Trudy had been fun for her, but it wasn't a reciprocal thing. "How'd you become a *chef*?"

"I went to school for it," she said, smashing the garlic with the flat of her knife and then dicing it into tiny pieces. She'd preserve it in oil, perfect shortcut for soups, stews and quick sautés.

"Why?"

She took a deep breath and considered her answer to a question no one had ever asked her. "I guess I've always wanted to be a chef. My grandmother and father were chefs and I spent a lot of time in the kitchen with them. I always really loved it."

He grunted, his eyes narrowed over the garlic clove in his pink hands.

"What do you want to do?" she asked.

"DJ," he answered quickly.

"Oh really?" she asked, again fighting the grin. "You like music?"

"I like parties."

"It might take more than that," she said.

"Maybe you can show me how to cook something and I'll see if I like that."

She blinked, taken aback. An apprentice. A fifteen-year-old juvenile-delinquent apprentice.

Stranger things had happened, she guessed.

"Okay," she said, "but you need to tell me what you got in trouble for."

"Max didn't tell you?" He asked.

"Max doesn't talk much. I don't know if you noticed."

Cameron grinned and went back to his peeling. "I missed a lot of school," he said. "Truancy or something."

"Why'd you miss school?"

He shrugged again, his face carved of stone. Her years

with Gabe had taught her not to push against people made of stone. She knew she wouldn't get any more from him.

"All right," she said. "When we finish this we can start work on the menu I've put together for the inn. Tonight we're trying it out."

The boy's muddy-brown eyes, usually downcast and sullen, sparkled with sudden interest and Alice felt an answering spark in her breast.

"Cool," he said and went to work double time. "Hey," he said after a moment. "Where are your kids?"

Her stomach fell to the floor. "Why..." She swallowed. "Why do you think I have kids."

"Because that's what adults do. They have kids. Don't they?"

"Not me." She smashed the flat of her knife down on the butcher block. "I don't have any."

"Too bad," he said as if it weren't devastating, as if his words, so casual and friendly, didn't lay waste to her. "You'd be good at it."

9

I t was perfect, the slow spin of satisfaction in her chest told her that. The bubble of joy in her throat confirmed it. Appetizer portions of the lunch menu and dinner salads sat, beautifully plated, ready to be served.

"All right, Cameron," she said—and because they'd worked hard together and he'd listened and only dropped one sandwich, which he ate, and because he seemed to really enjoy himself—she put her hand on his shoulder and gave it a squeeze. "Let's show 'em."

She grabbed three of the plates and left him with two. "You remember your lines?" She asked, turning backward to face him and opening the door with her butt.

"Spinach salad," he murmured, rehearsing. "Grapefruit vinegar—"

"Vinaigrette," she corrected.

"Grapefruit vinaigrette, blue cheese, egg and pine nuts."

"Not bad." She smiled at him and they stepped into the dark dining room.

The table she'd prepared was a small island of glittering light in the shadowed room. The three men sitting there looked up at her with expectation and happiness on their faces.

It was what every chef wanted to see when they stepped from kitchen to dining room. It was like being wrapped in a warm embrace, a victorious hug.

I love it, she thought, her throat choked with sudden pride. *I love it so much.*

She set down her first dish in front of Gabe because it was one of his favorites. "Grilled salmon salad with miso dressing," she said. "You have to share."

He grinned at her, his fork already poised to eat.

"Ham and white cheddar panini with sweet maple mustard." She set the plate down in front of Max, who groaned as if there were women performing sex acts on him.

"Thai chicken stir-fry," she said, placing the bowl under Patrick's eager nose. "With soba noodles."

She turned toward Cameron. In this light with everyone looking at him, the kid seemed suddenly so young. So vulnerable. Her heart hiccupped with pride and the old longing she had gazing at any child.

"Spinach salad," he said, placing the salad next to Max. The candle glow revealed his sudden nerves, his naked glance at Max who, she realized, might be more of a father figure than Cameron had ever had.

She stepped back out of sight and wiped her suddenly wet eyes on the sleeve of her jacket.

"It's got a bunch of stuff in it I can't remember," the boy admitted, looking toward her in the shadows apologetically.

"Looks good, kid," Max said and Cameron's chest puffed up. "Looks real good."

Cameron set down the carrot-ginger soup. "Enjoy," he said with an awkward little bow and came to stand at her side.

"We'll be back with the dinner entrées," she said and left the table of men as they began to eat.

"Oh dear God," Patrick sighed. "That's good."

"So's this," Max said. "Hey, get your fork away, I'm not done."

"You've done a great job, Alice," Gabe's voice floated through the dark room to wind around her. "Thank you."

"You're welcome." She slung her arm around Cameron's shoulder. "Great job," she whispered near his ear and quickly, briefly, his arm came across her waist in a sudden tight squeeze and then vanished.

Pride, relief, excitement, all combined in her, lifted her off her feet with a sensation that was unfamiliar.

I'm happy, she realized. *For the first time in five years, I'm happy.*

∿

"Why'd you leave her?" Max asked, using his finger to wipe up the last of the sour cherry sauce that had covered the duck.

Gabe pushed away from the table, too full to even answer.

"Yeah?" Patrick asked. "A woman who cooks like that and is—"

"Shut up," Gabe finally managed to say, though his command lacked enough heat to actually get them to stop talking.

Every single dish had been perfect. Max even ate the vegetarian pasta. Gabe needed to go back into the kitchen and tell Alice how good it had all been, but he didn't. He would, he told himself. In a minute. At the moment he needed to just sit here and marvel at the total fruition of all their plans.

Tonight it was as if they'd never split up. As if they'd gone seamlessly from that bedroom on Pape, sketching out their plans for this place to this moment, with the solid walls around them and the delicious food still perfuming the air.

Right now, with the sound of Alice's laughter creeping under the kitchen door, it was as if the bad stuff had never happened.

And that was dangerous.

"Alice was the right woman for the job," Max said. "It sure would be nice to get a little appreciation for having come up with that."

"Thank you," Patrick said and swung his eyes over to Gabe. "And you two seem to be behaving yourselves."

"We haven't killed each other, if that's what you mean."

"Good food and no bodies." Max stretched out his legs. "That's win-win."

His father's eyes didn't leave Gabe's face and he could practically read his thoughts. It would be better if they were fighting, and his father knew it. Gabe felt the pull of what had been good about them. He wanted to go into that kitchen and wrap his arms around her, kiss her just below the ear in that place that she loved, the way he once would have.

"I'm okay, Dad," he said. "It's all okay."

Patrick watched him a few minutes longer as if knowing he wasn't telling the whole truth before finally standing to gather the plates as he went.

"I'm going to go help them do the dishes."

"Yeah." Max stood, too. "I better get Cameron home since he missed the bus to help out."

"He's a good kid," Patrick said as they walked away from the island of light.

Gabe stared at the ceiling and wondered why, with everything going so well, so according to plan, he felt as though the ground beneath his feet was quicksand and he was in terrible danger of losing his balance.

∽

It was the scheduled late-afternoon Monday conference call and Alice's note-book was filled with the Crimpsons' wedding demands, which she'd tried to organize into lists and pages according to days. But as the call progressed and the demands kept coming, her attempts to organize it had fallen apart. Now she simply doodled pictures of a giant lizard wearing a veil, eating a woman. Chuckling, she sketched a little chef hat on the woman and showed it to Gabe, who laughed silently.

"We're sending you the boat we want filled with sushi," Gloria Crimpson, mother of Bridezilla screamed, clearly not understanding the basic function of speakerphones.

Alice stopped doodling.

"*Boat?*" She mouthed to Gabe in the silence of the office. "Did she say boat?"

"What kind of boat are we talking about?" Gabe asked, reading Alice's fears.

"It's a small rowboat."

"You want a rowboat filled with sushi?" Alice asked, just to clarify.

"Won't that be fantastic?" Savanah Crimpson said. "I mean, since we decided on a nautical theme..."

Alice threw her notebook in the air and sat back in her chair. "When?" she mouthed to Gabe. "When did we decide on a nautical theme?"

Gabe put his finger to his smiling lips and she wanted to kill three people—the Fish-Stick Queen, the progeny and her ex-husband who seemed to be delighting in this.

"We look forward to getting the rowboat. We need to know the final numbers so we can figure out just how much sushi we're going to need."

The numbers. The all-important numbers. A muscle twitched below Gabe's eye and Alice felt her own stress level start screaming for the roof. If the numbers were huge, the small hold they had on things would be blown and they'd need many more staff and tighter deadlines on food and—

"We've cut our guest list," Savanah said, an unheard-before iron edge to her voice.

"Sweetheart," Gloria wheedled. "We're still discussing this."

"No, Mom, we aren't." Gabe's eyebrows lifted and Alice crossed her fingers that perhaps the previously spineless bride had managed to remember she walked upright. "Our numbers are ninety-five."

Gabe's arms shot up in the air and Alice flopped back in her chair, a weary rag doll of relief. Ninety-five they could do. Easily.

The tension on the other end of the line was crushing and Alice was grateful when Gabe went to work with his charm.

"Savanah, we will put together a beautiful event for you and your guests. Ninety-five people will allow it to be personal and elegant and filled with your personality."

Alice choked on a laugh since the Fish-Stick Princess didn't seem to have a personality and Gabe shot her a control-yourself look.

"Now, when you say nautical theme, are you referring to food and decor?" he asked.

"Well," Savanah said, "since you said there were environmental laws against the pink swans..."

"Nice one," she mouthed to Gabe and he nodded.

"I think yes, maybe some anchors and—"

Alice shuddered.

"Savanah, my partner and I will put together a list of decoration options and a menu with your nautical theme and I will e-mail it to you by the end of the day."

"Tomorrow," Alice piped in, and Gabe scowled.

She shrugged, there was only so much she could do as a one-woman wedding planner.

"Wonderful," Savanah said.

"Gabe," Gloria added, "if the numbers change again, are we—"

"Your numbers have to be final by the end of day tomorrow," Alice chimed in. "I'm ordering food on Wednesday."

Gabe winced and she guessed she hadn't handled that as well as he would have.

"If we had more time," Alice said, "perhaps—"

Gabe slid a thumb across his throat, telling her to stop.

"Well, there isn't more time," Gloria said, her voice frigid. "My daughter—"

"The time frame is perfect. Trust me," Gabe said, leaning over the phone and pushing Alice out of the way. "We will put together a beautiful event."

A beautiful, small, quick event. Alice wondered if the Fish-Stick Princess was knocked up.

"We'll be coming in a week early," Gloria said. "With guests arriving two days before the wedding."

"We already have been getting reservations," Gabe said. "As I said when you contacted me, Gloria, there is no need to worry. You just need to check your e-mail and show up."

Everyone hung up and Alice and Gabe sat in the quiet of his office, staring at the phone.

"She's pregnant, isn't she?" she asked.

"Six months. She was going to elope, but her mom talked her into a quickie wedding."

"Can't have a Fish-Stick Bastard?"

Gabe laughed then fell silent. She could guess what was going through his mind—the same things that were going through hers.

"Anchors?" she asked, incredulous.

"What else says nautical?"

"We could trap some seagulls and have them crap all over—"

"Funny," he said, sitting back. "But not helpful."

She picked up her pencil and tapped it against the notebook.

"We could dress the waiters as pirates," she said, enjoying the look on Gabe's face. "Dunk tank?" She asked.

"Clearly, there is something about the Crimpson women that makes you a bit giddy," he said. "Other than flooding the place, or hanging anchors from the ceiling, what can we do?"

"Let me sleep on it," she said, stretching.

"Ah, yes, the famous Alice 'it came to me in a dream' solution." He wasn't mocking her, his eyes were warm and his body relaxed. She realized that she hadn't seen him this comfortable around her in years.

"Hey, it saved your ass a few times," she said. "Remember that corporate—"

"Of course," he groaned. "Of course. And if I remember correctly, I thanked you, quite handsomely, for that."

As soon as he said it, Alice felt her face get hot, a flush built across her chest and up her face to her hairline. He'd surprised her with a trip to Mexico, an all-inclusive resort, and they'd lain on the beach and drunk fruity drinks and made love for a week straight.

It was the first time she'd gotten pregnant. The only time without the help of doctors. She'd miscarried at twenty weeks, just after their wedding.

"I'm starving," Gabe said, standing so fast his chair spun out and hit the wall behind him. She looked up at him, watched the nervous energy radiate off him like radioactive rays. He remembered, too, and it made him uncomfortable.

His discomfort with their history used to make her angry. It made her want to fight and wound him for his coldness, for his uncaring heart. But with the years came a new understanding of the man.

He wasn't cold. He was scared.

Not my problem, she thought, trying to control her wayward heart, which melted at this new understanding of her ex-husband. *It's not my job to fix this man anymore. I was never good at it anyway.*

"Ham sandwich?" she asked, knowing his weaknesses.

"With white cheddar?"

"Like I'd put together a ham sandwich with anything else," she scoffed, and led him from the office into her kitchen, where, as always, things were in balance.

She never let her kitchen get messed up with personal things. It was bad chi...or whatever.

Even the bad memory of Gabe trying to fire her almost

two weeks ago had been replaced by the rolling out of the inn menu with Cameron's enthusiastic help.

In her kitchen she and Gabe could discuss work, be friendly, laugh, even, as though the past were not between them. But nothing too personal, nothing too painful, nothing that would sully this beautiful room where she spent all her days—those topics were strictly off-limits.

He pulled up the stool where Cameron had been camped out for the past three days.

"So how are things working with the kid?" Gabe asked, leaning against the counter. "Max said you haven't kicked him out of the kitchen yet."

Alice pulled the ingredients for the ham sandwiches out of the fridge then slid open the big heavy drawer she was using as a breadbasket and grabbed the baguette Cameron had attempted to bake yesterday. Tasted fine. Looked terrible.

"Pretty well," she said. "He's very keen. He did a great job Friday night."

"I couldn't believe it when he came out those doors carrying plates with you. He didn't even look like the same kid."

"Well, pulling his hair back helped."

"That's great, Alice. I mean great that you found a little help—"

"I don't know how much he's helping," she said, grinning at him over her shoulder. But the arrangement was good for both of them, her and Cameron. He filled the room with empty chatter that saved her from thinking too much, and he listened to her when she explained something, which made her feel as though she was contributing to something besides the destruction of her liver. He'd learned how to hold a knife confidently and how to check when duck was done or when carrot-ginger soup needed more salt.

She got to watch the pallid sullen look around his eyes vanish and his gray complexion turn pink.

Another patient healed by her kitchen.

"Well, it's got to be a good thing for him," Gabe said, plucking a slice of cheese from the stack she'd cut. "The kid doesn't have any positive role models, that's for sure."

"What's his story?" she asked, spreading maple mustard on the misshapen slices of bread. "He says his folks don't care about him, but I can't tell if that's just him being a teenager or if it's real."

"I'm pretty sure it's real. The mom's gone, the dad drinks." He shrugged. "They live way out in the country and if his dad is too drunk to get Cameron to school he misses school, which is what landed him in trouble. I don't think he's in danger of going to juvie. I think they want to remove him from his home."

Her heart sank for Cameron. "The kid is bright, he should have a shot at school."

"I know."

Silence reigned and soon it became too heavy. Sunset was about a half hour away and the shadows were growing long in the kitchen. It was her favorite time of day, quiet and special.

And somehow, either by his quiet or the feel of his gaze on her back, she knew in her bones Gabe was remembering that and it created a hushed intimacy between them. Two weeks before, the truce wouldn't have been there.

Her spacious healing kitchen was becoming smaller with every breath.

But there was nothing to stop the rush of good memories, the little sweet details they remembered about each other. Her favorite time of day. The way he liked his ham sandwiches. Five years ago she'd do this for him and place the sandwich in front of him with a kiss and he'd pat her bottom every time she was in reach and it would be a good thing. And right now, in her kitchen at her favorite time of day she missed that closeness with a physical pain.

And frankly it scared the bejesus out of her. She felt a little naked without her anger. Defenseless without her resentment.

"Lettuce?" she asked needlessly, as if she hadn't made him a thousand ham sandwiches, but she needed to put the distance between them. Needed to pretend she didn't remember him as well as she did, to pretend her life truly had gone on without him.

"God, no." He pretended to shudder.

She slid the plate across the butcher's block toward him and leaned against the counter with her own sandwich. "So," she said, "the nautical food is easy. Lobster tail and filet?"

He shook his head, turning up his nose. "How many weddings have you been to with that on the menu?" he asked. "And frankly, my serving staff isn't that plentiful, or well trained for table service."

She nodded, he was right.

"How about stations?" he asked. "You know we have the sushi boat and perhaps some oysters and we could have another station with paella?"

"And a grill station with fish, and we've got to have a meat option." She grabbed his wavelength. "We could do portobello mushrooms for the vegetarians."

"Excellent. Some cheese and crudités—"

"And dessert," she said, smiling. "Done and done."

"You're going to need some trained chefs to handle those stations," he said. "And I don't—"

"I'll ask my folks." Her father was trained, her mother was simply an excellent cook. They couldn't ask for better. "They'll think it's a hoot."

"*A hoot?*" Gabe swallowed audibly and she smiled at him.

"They've forgiven you for knocking up their only daughter."

"You sure? Because those Christmases at their house were pretty chilly."

"Right." She laughed. "The way they showered you with gifts and that homemade eggnog only you loved? Yeah, they hated you." After her folks had gotten over the initial whirlwind of her and Gabe meeting, falling in love, falling in bed, getting pregnant and getting married, they'd done their part and fallen for Gabe in a big way. The divorce had hit them pretty hard.

"They'd love to help you out," she said. "And they're cheap."

"Perfect. How quick can you get me a budget?" he asked.

"Tomorrow."

"Sounds good." He nodded at her, his smile electric, and she faced it head-on before it got too uncomfortable. She wished he were a stranger. But then they wouldn't work together this well. Every situation had its own catch-22.

"Can I ask you a question?"

"Sure," she said, "I can't guarantee I'll answer it."

"What happened with Zinnia?" He put down his sandwich and watched her.

She avoided his eyes. There was nothing wrong with talking about it, she tried to convince herself, but it still wasn't easy to open her mouth and let the words come out.

"Bad management on my part," she said. "I'm a good chef but a lousy businesswoman."

"Was it because of the drinking?" he asked.

She shook her head. She couldn't even pretend to be angry for some reason. Her kitchen took all the heat out of her, plucked her righteous indignation away like a feather. "I wasn't drinking that much then." The words stuck in her throat like a fishbone. She hadn't told anyone this, largely because no one really cared to ask. Restaurants failed all the time; no one except Gabe would understand that hers shouldn't have. "I just trusted the wrong people. I was so used to working with you." She smiled at him briefly, looking through her lashes at his solemn expression that he never realized was more attractive than all his grins. "I didn't watch my manager closely enough, or my accountant, for that matter. We bled money, and by the time I realized it, my accountant was gone and my manager had gotten a new job and I was left with a lot of debt."

"I can't imagine how hard that must have been," he said, his voice and the look in his eyes a loving stroke to her pride. This was the man who had listened to all of her dreams, stroked away those early tears before they were both flooded. This was the man who bolstered her when she was down, made her rest when she was weary and told her, every day, how special she was.

She busied herself wrapping the bread and putting it away so she wouldn't do something stupid such as reach out for him.

What happened? part of her howled. Where did that man go? She'd forgotten about him, lost him in the years that followed their string of tragedies.

"It was hard," she said. Stupidly, tears burned behind her eyes and she would have sworn she'd cried all she could for Zinnia. "The divorce and losing the restaurant—" She took a deep breath, mortified when it shuddered in her chest. "It was a pretty powerful one-two punch."

On top of the miscarriages, she didn't add, because he'd leave and suddenly she didn't want that. She hadn't just lost her husband in the divorce, she'd lost her very best friend. Her partner. A person who understood her inside and out.

And right now, in her warm and beautiful kitchen, she missed him. She missed Gabe, her husband, best friend and partner. The scrape of his stool against the terra-cotta tiles was like a low growl.

She could feel him—in her skin and along her nerve endings—approaching her.

"Hey," he whispered and she looked up to find him a breath away from her.

His hand brushed her arm, pushed back the black hair that had slipped from her bun. "I'm so sorry," he said.

She swallowed, unable to speak, unable to breathe because there was no air in the room.

Her eyes met his and the heat in those beautiful familiar blue depths melted her bones, her resolve, her better sense. So when he put his arms around her, she collapsed willingly into his chest, finding that familiar place under his chin to rest her head.

She slid her arms around his back as though the past five years hadn't happened, as though she still had the right to his touch, his long strong embraces.

She closed her eyes and, with a sweet piercing ache, she let her body be reminded of his.

"Alice," he murmured and she looked up, knowing how far away his mouth would be, knowing the stormy depths of those eyes and knowing that what she'd see there—confusion and desire—was the same thing he'd see in hers.

"This is a mistake," he breathed across her lips.

"I know."

But they did it anyway. Slowly, like magnets across a small space, their lips found each other's. She sighed at the touch, at his remembered taste, and he pulled her closer still while their kiss remained careful, chaste.

The sound of the outside doorknob turning shattered the reverent cocoon of her kitchen, and Alice hurled herself away from Gabe.

She expected Max or Patrick to walk in and she put cool hands over her hot face.

What would she say to them?

What would Gabe say?

With trembling hands and pounding heart she packaged up the homemade ham.

The outside door stuck and finally pushed open to reveal, not her ex-in-laws, but Daphne and Helen bathed in the gorgeous light of sunset.

Gabe was rarely caught speechless. Almost never since the divorce. But looking at Daphne and Helen in that doorway, while his body still screamed for Alice, literally struck him dumb.

"Hi," Daphne said, her wide eyes taking it all in.

"Hello, ladies," he finally said, forcing a smile.

"You told us to come watch the sunset here," Helen reminded him, unaware of the treacherous adult undercurrents swirling around the kitchen. "You said this was the best place in the world for that. So we're here." She hopped forward in her bright pink galoshes and Gabe's heart staggered and paused.

Right. Date two with Daphne. A sunset hike to the Hudson. Yesterday that had seemed like a good idea, but watching Alice from the corner of his eye blanche and brace herself momentarily against the fridge, he cursed himself.

"Is this a bad time?" Daphne asked, her face bland but her eyes piercing. She was no fool and wasn't about to be played like one.

He did not know what to do. How to make this right. He glanced at Alice, searching for some clue, some hint of how to not hurt her.

Hurt her? he suddenly thought. *She's my ex-wife and we made a mistake. There's no hurt here. There's just a mistake.*

That justification seemed right. How could they be hurt if days ago they were screaming at each other? They'd gotten caught up in working together. That's all. Talking about Zinnia and the divorce in a darkened warm kitchen had allowed them to forget for one brief moment that the past was best left in the past. That's all.

"No," he finally said, pushing Alice and the disaster of that kiss away. "This is a perfect time." He took a deep breath, willing Alice to understand what he so clearly knew to be the truth. The kiss was a onetime mistake. "You good?" he asked Alice. "I mean for the budgets?"

"No problem," she said, her head buried in the fridge. "Have a good time."

He smiled at Daphne, held out his hands and ushered them back out the door. "Let's go for a walk," he said, hoping he'd done the right thing but feeling Alice at his back like a burning fire.

10

"Hey, run on ahead, Helen, and see if you can find me some river rocks for the porch," Daphne said. The words weren't even totally out of her mouth before Helen was just a flash of pink and blond ponytail behind the bend in the river.

Uh-oh, Gabe thought, carefully pulling the fronds from the center stem of a fern leaf he'd plucked to keep his hands busy. His stomach churned in knots. There were words, explanations to Daphne, to Alice, to all of them knocking at his teeth and he worried that if he opened his mouth, he might say something dumb such as, "I kissed my ex-wife because I like her. I like her but she's like poison to me."

He worried that if he opened his mouth he'd turn to this wonderful woman and say, "I am so confused."

Not exactly the right thing to say on a date.

"Gabe, I don't know what's going on with your chef, but we interrupted something tonight and I think—"

"Alice is my ex-wife."

There. I said it.

He felt some of the knots loosen in his stomach.

Her mouth hung open for a second, then shut as she digested what he'd said. "Are you in the process of getting back together?" she asked.

"We are in the process of—" He stopped, unsure. "Working together."

"That's all? Because it didn't look like you were just working together. And that's fine." She held out her hands as if she had given up any interest she had in the situation and he didn't want that. He wanted her interest. He liked her, he really did. She was a potential future while Alice was and would always be the past.

Gabe grabbed her hand and stopped walking, turning her to face him.

"As a rule," she said, crossing her arms over her chest, her gray eyes shooting out sparks, "I don't date men who are still in love with their ex-wives."

He nearly laughed. Still in love with Alice? Good God, he hoped he wasn't that dumb. "I am not still in love with Alice. She's had a rough go of it lately and tonight she finally talked about it." He took a deep breath. "Things got emotional on both sides, but there is nothing going on with her. I swear it."

Daphne studied him, the intelligence in her eyes made him uncomfortable, as if she could see truth that he didn't.

"Why did you split up?" she asked.

"Why does anyone split up?" he asked, as if all couples, in some deep place, shared the same reasons.

"My husband and I wanted different things," she said. "He thought living a simple life out on a farm was what he wanted. Two years in he changed his mind." She shrugged. "I figure I should have seen it coming."

He shook his head. "Alice and I wanted the same things."

Family. Home. A tribe of our own. "We just couldn't give it to each other."

He tossed the frond. "I needed a chef and she needed a job and it seemed like it could work."

"It's not?" Daphne asked.

He stepped forward, away from her eyes, tired of being questioned for the truth. "No, it is. It's working out fine." *Better than fine, it's like the dream we had a million years ago. Better even than that.* Kisses at dusk, troubled kids working out their problems in the kitchen, weddings being planned —there was nothing he could ask for that would be better. Except...if his chef wasn't Alice. If his blood didn't hum for his ex-wife. If it was another woman with whom these two months could actually build into something more. Then it would be perfect. There was no chance of that with Alice. "I should have been prepared for that as much as I was prepared for it not working out."

"What was the thing you couldn't give each other?" Daphne asked.

His throat was tight. Thick. And he didn't know where this emotion had sprung from. "Children," he finally managed to say.

"What happened? Was she—"

"I'll tell you, Daphne. Someday. Just not today." When Alice wasn't here. He could tell Daphne was dissatisfied by that answer. She was a good woman who deserved more, but that was as much as he could give her.

Alice would kill him if she knew he was talking with Daphne about the things he could never to talk to her about.

They continued walking, the sound of Helen ahead of them like a lighthouse in a dark night. And just when he'd controlled the unruly ends of his emotions, Daphne slipped her hand in his, her fingers brushed his, and her grip, true and firm, a warm surprise, held him strong.

Alice closed her eyes behind her sunglasses and rested her head against the tree at her back. It was nearly 3:00 p.m. and she could not muster any enthusiasm for baking. None.

Chocolate turned her stomach, the smell of lemons made her gag, everything was too bright and looked too rich. She didn't want to touch food. Or smell it.

She took a sip of coffee and her stomach nearly rebelled.

The demons had run her ragged last night.

And she was paying the price today.

At some point in the middle of that bottle of wine she'd realized what had gone wrong; her mantra had changed over the last two weeks. She'd gone—subtly and in small steps—from not wanting anything, to wanting everything. It had started with the kitchen, and the food, and Cameron. Then she'd started wanting to make more decisions, she wanted to impress her ex-husband, Max and Patrick. She wanted everything she touched to be perfect, yet two weeks ago she'd been grilling grade-B steak at a chain restaurant so she would never want anything. So that she couldn't long for perfection.

She'd kissed Gabe last night. She'd kissed him because she wanted him. And there's no telling where that would lead. Sex? Wanting to try again? Try again to have a baby? Try again to be a family?

Those were ridiculous notions, suicidal. She couldn't survive another go-around with Gabe even if she wanted it

—which she didn't. And, more to the point, it was very obvious from the way he walked away from her last night that he didn't want it.

So what am I doing? She wondered. *Why am I feeling so crappy?*

This morning she practiced her old mantra, the one that made it possible for her to wake up in the morning and not weep for all that she couldn't have.

There is nothing I want.

There is nothing I need.

"Hey, Alice!" Cameron jogged up the small hill to where she sat overlooking the parking lot and the trailhead Max had so carefully made. "I looked for you in the kitchen," he said. He looked like a puppy, floppy brown hair and an overeager smile.

"I'm not there," she said, managing to surprise herself with the flatness in her voice, the harsh edge to her words.

"Yeah." The overeager smile fled. "I figured."

He watched her for a minute, the look in his eyes slowly changing, slowly reverting to the hard, who-gives-a-shit kid he'd been over a week ago, and she hated that she had so much influence over him. That what she said or did mattered so much.

I want to be alone, she thought. *I just want to be alone.*

"What's the matter with you?" he asked, his sneer creeping back onto his mouth.

She didn't answer. She didn't *have* an answer. Heartsick and stupid? Foolish and hungover? Tired and battered? Kissed and forgotten.

"You're working with Max today," she said instead.

"But—"

Oh, God. The wounded look in his eyes shattered her and she had to look away.

"You said we were working on desserts."

"Well, it's complicated." She pushed herself to her feet. "It's better if I do it by myself."

She walked by him, the ground uneven, and she stumbled slightly. "You're drunk," he snapped and his tone froze her. Such vivid loathing was something she only heard in her own voice.

Cameron ran away, down the hill, across the parking lot and onto the trail, probably toward Max. She figured it was for the best.

She swallowed the last of her coffee, hoping it would wash away the taste of self-loathing and headed back to her kitchen.

The door swung open before she put her hand on the knob and she stepped out of the way as Gabe came storming out. He stopped, just shy of touching her.

"I was looking for you," he said. "I wanted—"

"It was a mistake," she said, glad for her sunglasses so he couldn't see her eyes. "It won't happen again."

"But—"

Ice filled her veins and she understood why Gabe froze her out so much. It felt good to feel nothing.

To not be responsible for someone else's pain.

"You get your wish, Gabe. We'll never talk about it again. I won't wallow and you can pretend it didn't happen. And in a month and a half you'll never have to see me again."

He swallowed, his strong throat flexing and relaxing. Her belly coiled with tension of all sorts. She took a step away, hoping distance would help her breathe, would help her body relax, but it didn't. She could still feel him there, just out of touch.

"I wanted to tell you we're having a staff meeting this afternoon," he said finally.

She didn't even feel embarrassed, she was that cold. "Fine," she said and blew past him.

"Our first guests arrive on Thursday," Gabe said, looking out at his staff, which included his dad, brother, ex-wife and four women and three men who'd answered his ad to help clean and serve food to the guests.

"We have two couples coming from Canada, Joy Pinter from *Bon Appetit* and Marcus Schlein from *New York Magazine*." His hired staff paid attention, but his chef seemed wildly distracted. Alice stared at him, or rather through him, as if he wasn't here, as if he was just a voice from the heavens. The breeze that blew from her was icy cold and that worried him. It worried him that she looked more like the woman he'd met behind Johnny O's than the woman who drew funny pictures of giant lizards for his amusement, than the woman he'd kissed last night.

He'd awoken this morning like an amputee searching for a missing limb, patting down the side of the bed he'd never stopped thinking of as hers. He'd dreamed of her with him, in his bed, her slight snores, the way she mumbled kitchen lists, the sweet swell of her backside pressed into the cradle of his hips, the smell and feel of her hair across his pillow, because she'd always slept better close to him.

He'd tried to forget the dream, but his chest and arms felt the phantom shape of her against him, no matter how much he tried to think of Daphne.

Oh, man, this is a mess.

A mess made worse by his father mooning around like

some teenager for a woman who'd left him to raise two small boys by himself over thirty years ago. Gabe knew Dad wanted to talk about it, but what the hell was he supposed to do? She'd left and Gabe wasn't about to start talking about her now as if she'd never been gone at all.

His stomach was in knots, his head ached, and his hand, which had been held by Daphne, burned as much as his lips, which longed to kiss Alice.

Such a mess. A disastrous mess.

A little more than a month, that's all they had to get through. Then the wedding would be over and Alice would be gone. It didn't matter that this was the most important month of his career.

"I've written all their arrival and departure dates, the cottages they will be staying at and any dietary concerns they have." He handed out the papers he'd copied, and his staff, except for his family, looked at it.

"Is everyone ready for this?" he barked. "Opening weekend, we have two huge magazines—"

"We're ready, Gabe. Relax," Max said, and turned to Alice. "Have you seen Cameron today?"

"Yeah, about three," she said, folding up the paper without even reading it, which meant she didn't know one of the couples from Canada was vegetarian with a milk allergy.

Wonderful. Great. This is going to go so well.

"I sent him to you," she said and stood as if they were done.

"He didn't come to me," Max said. "Why didn't you let me know your change of plans?"

"I didn't know I had to." Her voice was lifeless as she walked away.

"Alice," Gabe called, trying to keep his temper in check. "Joy and Marcus will want to interview you."

"Fine."

He took a deep breath. "It would mean a lot if you'd pretend to be human rather than a—"

"I said *fine*," she repeated.

He stared at the ceiling and counted to twenty.

"What happened to her?" Max asked. "One minute she and Cameron are thick as thieves and the next she's...like that."

Gabe knew of course. He'd kissed her. He'd kissed her and then gone on a date with another woman.

"I'll fix it," he said and Patrick laughed.

"What?" he snapped at his father.

"There you go again, thinking you can finesse everything," he said.

"I'm not finessing anything. Alice is angry with me and I'm going to fix it."

"How?"

"I don't know how!" he snapped. *I never knew how. I still don't. I can't fix her.* "I'll think of something."

"When your mother was mad at me she would only get madder if I tried to bring her flowers. I always had to—"

"I can't handle this," Gabe said to his brother. Max nodded and held a hand up at hip level. *I got it*, that gesture said, and Gabe thanked his lucky stars that Max was here.

"Has Mom been in touch with you, Dad?" Max asked when Gabe would have told his dad for the hundredth time to shut up. "Is that what all this is about?"

Patrick didn't say anything, his blue eyes said it all, and Gabe fell back in his chair, as though he'd been blown down by a stiff wind.

Mom had contacted Dad.

He couldn't even get his head around it. After he'd realized that Mom wasn't on a vacation, that making her pancakes that got cold every morning wasn't going to lure her back into their lives, he'd forced himself to think of her as dead.

But here she was, brought back to life.

"What does she want?" Max asked.

"To see you," Patrick whispered.

"Forget it," Gabe said, trying to get his legs under him. "We don't want to see her."

"I know," Patrick said.

"What the hell is wrong with you, Dad?" Gabe asked, finding a vent for all of his pent-up anger and confusion. "She left us. She left you thirty years ago and never came back and now you're acting like some lovesick kid? I don't get it."

"Me, neither," Max agreed in a much quieter voice.

Patrick finally looked up, his eyes wet but burning with some dark emotion that made both Gabe and Max lean away or risk being scorched by his gaze.

"You don't get to pick who you love," he said. He looked right at Gabe, right into his heart. "Do you, son?"

"You're wrong," Gabe said, feeling a soothing cold wave of anger cover him. "You can control that, you can control yourself."

Patrick laughed at him. "You're doing a great job of that son. Wanting to want Daphne while you've got your wife—"

"She's my ex-wife, Dad."

"Paper doesn't change things, Gabe."

"Wait, wait." Max held up his hands. "Are you saying you still love Mom, Dad?" Max asked, looking as baffled as Gabe felt. "After all these years, after never hearing from—"

"She's your mother," Patrick said. "She's my wife."

"No," Gabe said, standing. "She isn't, she hasn't been for years. We don't want to see her."

He walked away, furious. Furious with his father, with Alice, with his long-gone mother and with himself.

How am I going to fix this? he wondered, his head spinning. *How do I make all of this right?*

~

During the last days of their marriage Gabe had loved to tell Alice she was a glutton for punishment. He used to say she could teach self-flagellation to a monk. It was tiring, he told her, living with a woman so happy to wallow in her misery.

Sitting in her car outside Athens Organics she realized Gabe was right.

What the hell is wrong with me? she wondered, ignoring the dog that sat, panting outside her open car window. This is high-school stalker stuff.

She had a list of things she needed considering the two vegetarian Canadians coming this weekend, but she could have called in the order and had it delivered, allowing her to never see Daphne's and Helen's pretty, wide-eyed happy faces ever again.

But no—she shook her head—*I had to be sick about it.*

She realized how stupid this was and quickly put the car in Reverse to leave before she was seen. But she looked out her side window and saw Helen standing with the dog and Daphne behind her.

"Hi," Daphne said, shielding her eyes from the setting sun. "Did you need something?"

Therapy? Electroshock therapy? A friend? "Mushrooms," Alice finally said, putting the car in Park and turning off the ignition.

"Do you want to get out of the car?" she asked carefully, as though she knew what kind of mental case Alice really was.

Is it written on my face? Alice wondered.

"We're having smoothies," Helen said. "After-school snack. You want one?"

She nodded numbly as Helen's sweet voice sent arrows through her.

"Or a glass of wine," Daphne offered. "You look like you might need something stronger than blueberries and bananas."

Alice wiped her mouth with hands that shook and knew that at any moment she could be crying or screaming.

This is what working with Gabe had brought her to. She'd stopped feeling this way, she'd numbed the pain with alcohol and work she didn't care about. And now here it was all over again.

"I just need to pick up a few things for opening week-end." She took the list from the passenger's seat and opened the car door.

"Okay," Daphne said diplomatically, her eyes scanning the list. "We've got it all. I can just run down…" Daphne paused, her eyes flickering to her daughter then to Alice and, in that moment, that brief gap, Alice knew Gabe, who would never talk to her, had talked to Daphne about the babies.

The betrayal tore the breath from her body and she leaned against her car, suddenly feeling a million years old, everything about her too tired to keep pretending.

"Helen, can you go down to the hothouse and give Dan this list and ask him to bring the stuff up to the house?"

Daphne asked, sending her daughter away with a pat on the bottom.

The dog barked and took off for the fields after Helen, startling some bird nesting in the trees by the house. Daphne stared at Alice and she stared back, wondering what had possessed her to come here. And more important, what was possessing her to stay.

"Gabe said there is nothing between you," Daphne said.

Alice nearly laughed. "Nothing good," she said. "You don't need to worry."

Daphne smiled, but it was grim. "He said the reason you split up was because you wanted the same things but couldn't give it to each other."

"He was chatty," Alice said through clenched teeth.

"I had some questions, seeing as how he is supposed to be dating me." Daphne crossed her arms over her chest. "Would you agree with him? You couldn't give each other what you both wanted?"

"That about sums it up."

"That doesn't sound like a good enough reason to spilt up," she said. Alice rocked back, angered at this woman's presumption, angered that it was the same way she had felt at the beginning of the end, as though there should have been something they could do to save themselves. Then she'd learned better.

"Trust me," she said, getting her bearings. Maybe this was why she'd come here, to put it all into words, to sort out the reasons and track the fall of their marriage to someone who didn't have front-row seats.

Or to start a fight.

She wasn't sure yet.

"It was plenty good enough," she said. "We were young and headstrong and in the end we just couldn't give a shit."

Daphne smiled, warmer this time. "Now you sound like a divorced woman."

"Great," Alice said, not sure if she should laugh or cry. "I'd hate to get the vocabulary wrong."

"Are you here to tell me all the things wrong with Gabe?" Daphne tilted her head, her braid falling over her shoulder like a rope.

God, wouldn't that be nice, Alice thought. *Give the woman a little map to the dangers ahead.* But she shook her head. "He's a good guy," she said, surprising herself. Warmth bloomed in her chest as her heart was bombarded by memories of better days, when he was the best guy. "One of the best."

Daphne's eyes narrowed again and Alice wondered if she was giving away too much of herself. If this woman could see through all the years to the twenty-four-year-old woman who had loved Gabe so wholeheartedly.

Do I still? she wondered, hollow and scared. *Is that what's so wrong with me?*

"Gabe said you couldn't have children. I'm sorry," Daphne said. "What—"

"Two second-trimester miscarriages, thousands of dollars in doctor bills, a load of disappointment and no babies." The words poured out of her, like water from an upended pitcher. She couldn't control them or stop them and didn't want to.

She stared at the blazing ball of the setting sun until the tears that burned in her eyes turned to water and slid away.

How can this be so easy? She wondered. For years she'd held this stuff in, refused to discuss it except to punish Gabe who never wanted to talk about it. And now that it was gone...she felt taller. As if she'd grown in the last few minutes.

Her mom had told her she needed to embrace group

counseling, let it heal her, and at the time she'd wanted to tell everyone to leave her alone. But, now, this felt good.

"The doctors said for me to carry a baby to full term I would need to be on bed rest from about three months on and even that wasn't a guarantee. And I just..." she shook her head. "We couldn't afford it. I didn't believe it." The pain of the truth, that she might have caused her own tragedy, sliced through her over and over again. "And in the end it didn't matter. The last miscarriage did us in."

She stared at the sun for a long time, until her face got hot, her body, freed of all of its bitter underpinnings relaxed into something else, something less brittle, something human.

Blinking, she turned to face Daphne. "I'm not sure why I said any of that."

Daphne smiled. "I'm a stranger on a bus."

"A stranger dating my ex-husband."

"Do you want me to stop?" she asked, eyebrows raised.

Yes. Yes. I do. Until I'm gone. Until I can't see.

"Of course not," Alice said. "We split up five years ago. There's nothing between us."

Nothing. No marriage. No house. No family.

"How about that glass of wine?" Daphne asked.

"Just one," she said, ready to sit down with the devil for a drink. "I'm driving."

11

Gabe poured himself some peach smoothie from the silver pitcher and placed it back into its dish of ice. The silver pitchers had been Alice's idea. Another one of her great ideas.

Like the fresh frittata and the cinnamon rolls and the Swiss muesli in the silver bowl beside the pitcher.

He should tell her, of course, walk right over to where she sat at the corner table waiting for him and Marcus from *New York Magazine* for the first of their interviews. It was Sunday, the last day of the opening weekend and in a few hours all the guests would be gone, giving them time to prepare for the next arrivals.

Saying those words, compliments, empty or not, used to be so easy for him. A way to grease the wheels and keep things running smoothly between him and anyone he worked with.

He watched her drink from her coffee cup, brush the dark hair from the side of her face and he knew she was hungover. Had been the whole week. But it didn't stop her from working. She worked like a woman possessed, which was great for him.

So why do I feel so bad?

She's doing everything I need her to do. She's got a month left and then she's gone and she can self-destruct on her own time.

He knew part of it was guilt. A part of this situation had been brought on by him. By the kiss and Daphne. He understood that. But Alice had been blaming him for all the mistakes, all of her hurt feelings almost the entire time he'd known her.

How much more responsibility could he take?

"Gabe?" Lori Zinger and her husband, Ian, one of the Canadian couples, stood beside him dressed for a morning hike.

"Hi, guys. Everything okay?" Gabe asked, tearing his thoughts and gaze from Alice.

"Wonderful," Lori said emphatically. "We just wanted to let you know that we're going to come back later in the summer with some other friends. This place is such a find!"

Gabe smiled and asked them to just write the dates down and he'd give them a return-visitors' discount.

"Another reason to love the Riverview," Ian said, grabbing a cinnamon roll as he walked out the door.

Gabe picked up one of the carafes of coffee and his own smoothie, then walked over to where Alice sat, shielding her eyes from the morning sun.

"Hi," he said, pouring more coffee into her mug.

"Thanks," she muttered.

"Food looks great."

"People seem to like it," she said and took a sip of coffee.

"One of the Canadian couples is coming back later in the summer."

"That's good news for you."

Every word between them was coated in acid, and compliments weren't making it better. Maybe reminding her of their partnership, of the investment she had in this place, would return this tin woman, this robot, into something familiar.

"The drawing for the decorations was approved by the Crimpsons."

She nodded as if she couldn't care less.

He took a deep breath and tried to remember what his father said about how sometimes things couldn't be finessed, that sometimes he had to beg.

"You ready for the interview?"

She shrugged and he felt the banked fires of his temper flare. He sat down opposite her and leaned in, wanting to shake her, to rattle her until she cared, just a little bit, about what these interviews meant to him.

He opened his mouth to tell her how much he needed her on her game right now. That she could go back to being a ghost, to blaming him for everything, to drinking away her life—

"You can't fix this, Gabe," she said, her eyes bone dry and burning. "We already tried."

His anger sizzled and died in a shroud of white smoke. Her pain spoke to his—the confusion, the weariness of the fight in her voice and eyes—spoke to all those matching emotions in him.

And it seemed, even in this, in their defeat, they were joined.

"I take everything too personally and you…do, too." She rubbed her forehead. "You just don't know it. Or don't show it. Or…" She smiled, a shaky, trembling thing that tore at his guts. "I don't know anymore, Gabe. I only know…you can't fix us."

Him, of course, it was supposed to be up to him.

"I'm not responsible for this, Alice."

"Of course not, Gabe." She reached out and touched his hand, a small incendiary touch, and then her hands were tucked back in her lap while his flesh burned. He flexed his fingers to shake off the feeling. "You are only responsible when things go right."

"That's not fair," he protested, but he knew if his father were sitting here he'd be nodding his head in agreement.

"There's not much about any of this that's fair."

"Is it because of Monday night? After the conference call?" he asked, the words *when we kissed* lodged in his throat, the memory of it stuck in his head. Not so much the dry touch of her lips to his but the feel, the beautiful remembered feel, of his *wife* in his arms. He'd never realized how much he missed the perfect fit of her head under his chin until she was back there.

It was why he didn't want to talk about it. He could tell in the way she didn't meet his gaze, it was why she didn't want to talk about it, either.

"Is it because of Daphne?"

She sighed and shook her head. "It's me Gabe. It's—" She looked up at the ceiling, her elegant neck arched, the pale white of her skin pulsing with her heartbeat. He felt the same pulse in his body.

He wanted to push these feelings away, the smoky tendrils of connection, of understanding and of caring that still lingered around his heart, tying him to her. He wanted them gone so he could get on with his life.

"Every time I want more—" she swallowed, her voice a rasp "—every time I reach out for something I don't have..." She shook her head and tried to laugh and he nearly cringed at the heartbreaking rattle. "I'm just reminded of how much better it is to not want anything."

"What did you want that night in the kitchen?" he asked and the air between them was still. She didn't move, didn't blink. His heart didn't beat. His lungs didn't work.

What answer do I want? What am I doing even asking this?

He felt himself pushed toward the edge of some cliff. A cliff he'd gone over once before and had no business flirting with again.

"You, obviously." Her voice was a sigh and his heart thudded painfully in his chest. "I think I wanted what we had. Before everything went so wrong. Working together just reminded me of the good times."

"But I could never make you happy," he told her, repeating his bare-bones reason for leaving the marriage. His failure that haunted him and drove him away.

"It shouldn't have been your job," she said. "And I think we both expected it."

These were words they'd never spoken. The truth they'd hidden behind fights and anger and slammed doors.

"I just want you to be happy." He said, turned and came out with this suppressed wish. "That's all I've ever wanted."

"That's all I've ever wanted for you," she whispered. Her eyes were on his, the beautiful obsidian gaze, and he felt himself fall over that cliff again. Back into feeling something for this woman. "And I wish, so much, that I was the person who could make you happy, Gabe."

He sat back in his chair, a hole in his chest with a cold wind blowing through it.

"Alice!"

"Marcus!" Her face lit up, her eyes sparkled, and for a moment she was the Alice of a week ago, before the kiss, the Alice before the miscarriages. The wind whistling though his chest blew colder when he realized they were the same Alice. Happy Alice. Glowing Alice. Infectious and laughing. Alice in love.

Marcus hugged her, his hands trailing across her back. Alice grinned up at him.

"God," he said. "How long has it been?"

"Five years," she said.

"You look good." The way he said it made Gabe's ears perk up. As though she looked *good* good. Jealousy, unwanted and stupid, gripped him.

"Never thought I'd see you here," Marcus continued, gesturing at the cathedral ceilings. "I thought you were a bright lights kind of girl."

Ha! Gabe thought. *That's how well you know her.*

"A girl can't live in the city forever." She smiled. "Look at you, hotshot reviewer for *New York Magazine*."

"Well, you're partially to thank. You urged me to apply."

Alice smiled and assured him he would have found his way to New York City eventually.

Gabe let their words wash over him while he made every effort to shake the inappropriate jealousy. Was this how Alice felt when he left with Daphne? Even as he wondered, he knew she must have felt worse.

He suddenly was torn between smart and stupid, right and wrong, what he wanted and what he should want.

He missed Alice in love. He missed being the man to make her light up. And while he knew those days were behind him, he hated being the person responsible for taking the light out of her eyes.

He let the truth of what he needed to do sink in. He didn't expect it to make her happy again, but he'd at least be taking responsibility for the one thing he could control.

They were still connected, by the past, by their marriage,

by whatever lingering feelings had survived the carpet bombing of the divorce and, while she was here, he needed to respect that.

He took a deep breath. As soon as the interview was over he'd call Daphne.

~

Alice pulled the frozen cinnamon rolls from the freezer to thaw and proof on the counter overnight. Most of the guests were leaving tonight, but Joy Pinter from *Bon Appetit* was staying one more day in order to get a tour of the grounds from Gabe.

And Alice had noticed that Joy seemed to like her espresso hazelnut cinnamon rolls.

Max walked in the side door, looking every inch the cop he'd once been—stone-faced, straight backed and exuding a general displeasure, a disappointment directed right at her.

Guilt leaped in the pit of her stomach. She'd handled the Cameron thing all wrong, and if she were less of a wimp, she'd actually deal with it. She'd ask to bring him back to the kitchen. She could take it, she was tough. The conversation with Gabe this morning had actually moved some of her baggage so she could deal with other people. Such as Cameron.

"Cameron's been arrested," Max said and the cinnamon rolls fell from her hands to clatter on the floor.

"What?" she asked, her hands and feet numb.

"They've sentenced him to the group home in Coxsackie." Max flexed his shoulders as though being around her made him uncomfortable and she realized that she wasn't a wimp—

she was a coward, and the one who suffered was Cameron. "I thought you'd want to know," he said and turned for the door, as though he couldn't quite get out of her kitchen fast enough.

She wiped her face with a shaky hand. "What can I do, Max?"

"It's a little late to do anything."

She grabbed his arm, held him in place. "What can I do to make it right?" She shook her head. "I...God. I was so wrong to treat him that way."

Max watched her for a long time weighing, she was sure, her sincerity. "Well, we can't get him out. But you could visit."

An idea sprang up in the back of her head, one she might pay for in the long run but that was the nature of doing the right thing.

"All right." she picked up the cinnamon rolls. Scanned the counter and her mental to do list and figured she had three hours before she needed to be back. She untied her apron and set it on the chopping block. "You have time to drive up there?" she asked Max, and his lips lifted in the smallest smile.

"That's my girl," he said and Alice nearly crumbled. He didn't know how wrong he was.

~

Forty-five minutes later they pulled up to an old white farmhouse surrounded by modern outbuildings. One looked big enough to be a gymnasium and the other looked as if it might be dorms.

Alice didn't know what she expected, but a group of kids playing basketball in the parking lot wasn't quite it.

"It's a school," Max said. "School and dorms and treatment facility."

"Treatment for what?" she asked, watching the kids, who all wore khaki pants and white shirts and couldn't have been older than fourteen, scramble for the ball. A tall boy with short hair grabbed the ball and tossed it toward the basket, missing spectacularly.

"Alcohol and drugs," Max said, parking the car and turning off the ignition. "Let's go. We need to talk to the director before we can talk to Cameron."

"You think this will work?"

"I'm not sure. They often have work-release programs, but usually not so far away."

"If he just had a car, he could get to school."

"I know. Let's go see what we can do."

Alice had stones in her stomach. She knew she wasn't totally responsible for this, but she couldn't help feeling that her sudden change in the way she'd treated Cameron had led him here.

Max waved at the faculty member working the basketball game, and the tall kid with the short hair stopped running and watched them.

It was Cameron, hardly recognizable without his long hair and filthy, oversize clothes. Alice waved but he just watched her walk by.

The director was a kind man, unassuming but with two huge dragon tattoos up his arms. Alice explained her plan to hire Cameron in her kitchen and asked if it was okay. He wholeheartedly approved.

"He'll need a ride back and forth after class," he said.

"We don't have the staff to provide a chauffeur all the way out to the inn."

"We'll be able to work it out," Max said. "Don't worry."

"Worrying is my job, Max." The director laughed and gave Alice an empty classroom to use to talk to Cameron and then sent the secretary out to pull him from the game.

Alice waited in the room, looking at drawings of dogs and horses and mountains and homes that had been tacked on the walls.

She couldn't help the flutter of nerves, the kick of worry that he'd yell at her, or refuse to see her. That she wouldn't have a chance to try to make things right. It had been over a week since she'd seen him and it felt like a month.

The door banged open and Cameron stood there, fresh faced and angry in properly fitting clothes.

The mother instinct in her that had survived her efforts to drown it for the past five years sighed. *What a good-looking boy.*

"What do you want?" he asked, his face twisted in an ugly sneer.

"To apologize," she said. "Come in."

He hesitated for a moment, then stepped inside, the door sliding shut behind him. He watched her, offering her nothing, and she almost smiled, recognizing his behavior and his need to protect himself from her.

She had a Cameron inside of her—a small girl, petulant and hurt and scared. And she'd been letting her run things for far too long.

"I'm sorry you got arrested," she said.

"I didn't." Cameron shrugged. "The school sent these people to my house and they brought me here."

"Do you like it here?"

He shrugged. "I get to go to class and play basketball."

"Sounds good."

"What are you doing here?"

"I wanted to apologize for the way I acted last week."

"Apologies from drunks don't mean anything," he snapped and she felt as if she'd been blasted right between the eyes with shards of glass.

"Okay..." She sighed and steeled herself for his venom because she deserved it. "How about a job?"

He looked at her, made a rude noise and looked away, but quickly looked back at her. "What are you talking about?"

"We have a wedding coming up in a month and I need help in the kitchen."

"Peeling potatoes?" His eyes narrowed and she nearly smiled. He was so transparent, as she figured she had been this morning with Gabe. Wishing so much that she was different. That he was. That they could make it work between them, in some alternative universe.

She nodded. "Among other things. I'll pay you well enough that, when you turn sixteen, Max will go with you to buy a used car so you can get to school."

His mouth fell open and his shoulders slumped and for a moment she saw his eyes turn bright with a sudden flood of tears.

She could feel the hope and longing roll off him and slam into her chest. Breath was thick in her throat, her chest felt tight, but in a good way, as though she couldn't hold in all the things she felt for him. How glad she was she could help him. Gabe probably wouldn't approve of her hiring Cameron with part of her salary, but he had left it up to her. And this was her choice.

Wanting more for Cameron felt good. She'd start there, maybe, and work toward getting more for herself.

"No," he said, surprising the hell out of her.

"No? Why?"

He chewed on his lip and crossed his arms over his chest, revealing a sudden strength she'd hadn't expected. "I've had enough of drunks," he said. "I'm here now. My dad can't—" he stopped, his voice cracked, and Alice's heart, which she'd been sure had been broken and rubbed into the dust, clenched and tore. "I won't work for you if you're drinking," he said.

"I'm not drinking anymore," she said. The words, like birds startled from a tree, were a surprise. But she realized that if Gabe couldn't make her happy, she needed to do it herself, and not drinking was square one.

"Since when?" he asked, doubtful, probably having heard similar words from his father.

She swallowed her pride, a thick ball of it that did not go down easy. "Since right now."

Alice stepped toward him and he watched her sideways as she put out her hand to shake on the offer, sealing his chance at school and a future and her promise to stop drinking and work on being happy, on her own.

"I want to work the grill," he said, jerking his chin up.

"Not on your life."

"No potatoes."

She winced. "Sorry. There will be potatoes."

"A car?"

"A Max-approved car." She nodded, her hand still hovering in the space between them.

"All right," he said, his hand slapping hers so hard her palm stung. "You're on."

She bit back a gleeful bark, a strange crow of joy, and shook his hand. "We'll pick you up tomorrow."

12

Gabe had ended his share of relationships. Probably more than his share. More like his share, Alice's share and probably Max's share, too, since Max and Alice didn't seem to believe in ending things when they needed to be ended.

Even so, with all that practice, with his "it's not you it's me" speech refined to an art form, spending Wednesday evening telling Daphne that he couldn't see her anymore didn't go quite as he had planned.

She braced herself on one of the posts in the gazebo and laughed until tears rolled down her cheeks.

"Oh, I'm sorry." She sighed. "I am. This is just—" She started to laugh again and Gabe crossed his arms over his chest and waited, impatiently, for Daphne to stop laughing.

"Oh, this is perfect. Just my luck, you know?" Daphne pulled a tissue from her dark blue barn jacket and wiped her eyes. "My first time back out in the dating scene and I get involved with a guy who isn't over his ex-wife."

"This has nothing to do with Alice," he lied. Too many things right now were tied to Alice. Breaking up with

Daphne, the success of his inn, his dreams, his thoughts. He felt a resentment churn into the feelings he still had for Alice, the desire he felt when she touched him, when he saw her bent over the chopping block, the sun in her hair. "We are only working together."

Daphne tilted her head at him as though he were some misguided teenager. "Gabe, it's fine if you don't want to tell me the truth. I understand that. You and Alice have a right to your privacy, but you have to at least be honest with yourself."

"I am," he said, but he could tell she didn't believe it, and frankly, neither did he. "It's a proximity thing," he finally admitted. "She'll be gone in a month and my life will get back to normal. We just—" He kicked a rock on the worn path. "She's got this gravitational pull that I get sucked into every time I'm around."

"Then why fight it?" Daphne put her hand on his arm and with that touch and its total lack of electricity and heat he knew that even if Alice weren't here it would never work with Daphne. "Gabe, if my ex came back, nothing in my life would change. Helen would probably be happier, but I don't feel anything for him. I don't hate him, I don't still love him, nothing. He has no gravitational pull."

"You're lucky."

"No." Daphne's voice had bite and she grabbed him to face her. "You idiot. You're lucky and you don't get it. What I felt for Jake is gone. Vanished. Because it wasn't real. If you really love someone, really love them, those feelings may change but they don't go away."

The truth in her words rattled around in his head, stirred things up in his chest.

"We don't work," he whispered. "Outside of sex and the restaurant business, we've never worked."

"Then you're not trying," she said, patting his cheek. "Start with the sex and work out from there."

Through the window over the stove Alice surreptitiously watched Daphne leave.

"What are you doing?" Cameron asked, a sneak catching another sneak.

"I'm spying on Gabe," she said as Gabe slammed the driver's-side door of Daphne's beat-up truck and she drove out of the parking area.

"Aren't you an adult?" Cameron asked.

"Sometimes," Alice answered, ducking out of the way when Gabe started walking toward the kitchen. "Keep going on those pots," she said and Cameron scowled, hating his temporary job as dishwasher.

She whirled to the far work counter where she'd stacked the material she'd ordered for the Crimpson wedding, grabbed it and hit the door to the dining room running before Gabe entered the kitchen.

She was being a child, she knew that, spying on the guy and then leaving so she wouldn't have to talk to him for fear of what she might say.

Their conversation four days ago haunted her. A thousand times since those moments of naked honesty she'd wanted to turn to him and ask him, Why now? Why couldn't they have spoken that way while married? When they'd both so clearly needed it.

"Alice?"

Crap. He'd followed.

"Hi, Gabe," she said, setting the bundles of blue silk on a nearby table. "What's up?" She pretended to check the bundles, keeping her back to him, but his silence compelled her to turn. "Did Daphne—"

Looking at him, her words stopped, hung suspended in her throat. He was a man ravaged, dark eyed and stormy. Barely contained anger mixed with a desire they'd both been suppressing rolled off him like heat from a banked fire.

They'd been skirting this moment, pretending this heat between them wasn't happening.

Apparently, Gabe was no longer pretending.

Her treacherous body longed for this reckoning.

"Drop off the spinach?" She finished the question, her voice weak.

He shook his head, coming farther into the room until he stood next to her. His silence was like another person in the room, a person sucking in all the air, taking up all the space.

"How did the tour with Joy go on Monday?" She asked, playing with the hemmed edge of silk like an inspector.

"Fine." His voice was that low rumble of thunder, like a faraway storm gathering strength.

"You and Marcus sure seemed friendly," he said, sounding like a jealous ex-husband. Alice lifted her head, aware of a sudden change. A rise in temperature.

"We dated." His eyes flared. "It was brief," she said, moving from stroking the edges of the cloth to unfolding it, as though more industry on her part would help her breathe, or would speed up this conversation, so she could see where it would go.

"When?"

"After the divorce before he got the full-time job and moved to the city."

She handed him one edge of the material, the indigo edge that matched his eyes at this moment. "Take this," she said, unable to stand next to him, feeling the heat of him, smelling the spicy and warm scent of him—that had nothing to do with soap or fabric softener and had everything to do with him—and talk of the other people in their lives.

She stepped away, holding the silver edge of the cloth and it unfurled into a watercolor banner six feet long and ranging from indigo to violet, to royal blue and down the radiant spectrum.

"Pretty, isn't it?" she asked, to fill the room with some sound other than the odd pounding of her heart.

What do you want?

What are you doing here?

"Beautiful," he said. Again the distant thunder and she looked up at him, caught his eye and knew it wasn't the cloth he'd been talking about.

"Marcus asked me to meet him in the city for dinner some night," she said, throwing it between them like a shield, but it landed like a gauntlet and his hands fisted the fragile fabric.

"Are you going to?"

She shrugged. "Depends." These were the words she'd been scared of saying. These were the stupid steps toward ruin.

"On what?"

"On what Daphne was doing here."

There. She'd said it. She couldn't take the words back. They couldn't pretend the pink elephant that breathed desire in the middle of the room wasn't there.

"I broke it off."

"Why?"

"Same reason you're not going to dinner with Marcus."

The air crackled and hissed and practically smelled of sex. Six feet away from him and she knew he was hard, just as he'd know she was wet.

Oh, I love it. She loved him this way. Loved and hated him.

"Why's that?" she asked, cocking her head and playing her part, devastating though it would be.

He pulled on the fabric and stepped toward her, reeling her in and chasing her down, and she let it happen. She wanted it. Waited for it. Then there it was.

His lips, moist and hot against hers. This kiss wasn't tentative or careful, it was pained and angry. It was the unleashing of a thousand repressed kisses, a hundred long nights and dozens of mornings wishing he was there.

He wrapped her up in his arms and the silk, held her so close she couldn't move and she wouldn't have if she could.

"You're ruining my life," he said against her mouth, before biting her lips aggressively, the way she loved. His words stung, particularly since he was such a part of the rebuilding efforts of her life. But thought dried up and blew away as the temperature between their bodies flared.

She arched her hips against his, felt the ridge of his sex beneath his jeans and her body turned to mercury against his.

"What are we doing?" she asked as he pushed her against the table. "What—"

"I don't care," he muttered against her throat, his hand sliding up her thigh to her hips. "I don't want to stop."

Yes. Right. No stopping. She opened her legs and he stepped between them, their dance as familiar as if they'd done this yesterday. His hands fisted in her hair and she sucked on the skin of his throat, used her teeth on his ear and every groan, every sigh and hiss from their lips threw gasoline on the fire between them.

The uncomfortable clearing of a throat behind Gabe didn't stop them. Barely slowed them down.

"For God's sake, son, you're in the dining room!" Patrick's hoarse bark doused them like ice water and Gabe stepped away, his hand on her elbow. She rose from the table and turned to pick up the banner, blushing like a sixteen-year-old, but she couldn't move, thanks to being wrapped up in the silk. She struggled her way free.

"Hi...Dad." Gabe said, smiling. They'd been caught making out by his father and Gabe was smiling.

Which, despite her general embarrassment and confusion, made her smile, then, oddly enough, laugh. Gabe watched her sideways and his lips twitched before he laughed, too. Patrick watched them as though he'd stumbled down the rabbit hole.

"You two are nuts!" Patrick said. "You always have been."

"That explains a lot," Gabe murmured, bending to help her pick up the material.

"You better know what you're doing, Gabe," Patrick said. "Because I remember what you were like the last time you guys wrecked each other, and I don't want to see you that way again." Patrick left, muttering and stomping his way to the kitchen.

That sobered Alice and she searched Gabe's handsome face for some twitch of emotion. "What were you like?" she asked, their faces so close she felt his warm breath on her cheek.

"A mess," he said and swallowed. "I loved you, Alice. I wanted to make it work."

His words flayed her, paralyzed her. Tears trembled on her eyelashes and she wiped them away before they fell.

"I can't..." He sighed. "I can't go through that again. This
—" his hand swirled between them "—whatever this is
between us, it's not a second chance. I can't survive a second
chance, not if it's going to fail."

"Me, neither," she said.

Neither one of them asked why it would have to fail,
though the words nearly leaped from her mouth.

"So?" His eyes bored into hers. "What was that?" he
asked, referring to their kiss and near-tabletop lovemaking.

"It was good, Gabe." She smiled and stroked his cheek.
"Maybe it's better to say goodbye this way, to end our relationship like this rather than the way we did five years ago."

"You mean the plate fight?"

"We did some damage." She nodded. "But I think what
we had deserves better than that." She got lost in the depths
of Gabe's eyes, lost there among the swirl of affection and
memory of desire, just barely contained.

"I need—" He covered her hand with his, the rough skin
on his palms sending sparks through her body.

Me.

Us.

To get naked. To kiss you. To love you.

"I need some time to think."

She pulled her hand free of his. Part of her hurt knowing
that she was so toxic, such a risk, that involvement—even
only physical—was not something anyone took lightly. But
part of her understood and appreciated the chance to think.
"And I need time to hang these silks."

The cool air blowing between them vanquished the last
of the fire they'd built with their bodies.

"You need help?" he asked.

"I do, but that's why your dad was here. He volunteered
to help me get the lighting up and ready."

"I'll send him back in." He tucked his hands in the pockets of his worn jeans and spoke louder in a near yell. "I'm sure he and Max are listening on the other side of the door."

"We can barely hear you!" Max yelled through the kitchen door, confirming Gabe's words. "You need to speak up!"

Alice felt emotion pulse through her body, longing and gratitude and regret that she no longer had a permanent place with these men.

"Bye," she whispered with a smile she knew would seem sad, but she couldn't pretend otherwise.

"Bye." He nodded, turned and left her alone with silk the color of his eyes ruined with her tears.

She and Patrick stayed up late building frames for the material. He'd been persistent with his questions, which she knew were born of concern, but she dodged them as best she could.

"I don't want to see you two hurt again," he said.

"Me, neither." She bent the thin light strips of pine in an effort to make the silk billow like waves. But all the wood did was crack. She swore and removed the splintered wood from the frame.

"Are you still in love?" he asked and Alice hung her head backward, examining the ceiling so she wouldn't have to look at her ex-father-in-law's knowing face.

"In love?" she asked the ceiling. "I don't know. I still love him. I think he still loves me, but that doesn't mean things will work," she said. "We loved each other last time, too."

Patrick grunted and hammered the finishing nails into the left corner of the six-foot structure. "I loved his mother," he said.

She sighed in relief. Finally the heat was off her and Gabe.

"I loved her so much that when she left I hated her."

"I know that feeling," she said, having experienced it for a number of years.

"I loved her so much that I hated her and I wanted her punished."

"Sounds familiar."

"So when she asked to come back I said no."

"That's about—" She looked up at him, her stomach in her knees. "What?"

"She asked to come back, twice. Well, three times."

"When?" she whispered.

"Three months after she left, then a year after that and now."

Her head reeled, she sat hard on her butt. "Do the boys know?"

"They know she's been in touch recently," he said and shook his head. "But not about her earlier letters."

"What?" She hardly knew what questions to ask, where to start. "Why?"

"Why?" He took a deep breath and let it out slowly. "Because I was a fool. Because I was scared. Because I was angry. Because, the truth was, life got easier without her. With just us."

I'm scared, her heart spoke. *I'm scared of Gabe breaking me all over again.* And she'd spent much of the last decade being angry.

God, I've wasted so much time.

"What are you going to do?" she asked him.

"What *can* I do? She wants to see them and the boys will barely even talk about her." He shrugged. "I don't want anyone to be hurt."

"What about you? What do you want?"

"I want my family together." His voice cracked and he hammered at the frame as if it were an animal trying to eat him.

"You should do it. Tell her to come here," she said, bold and gutsy because she'd be long gone. "Gabe and Max need to deal with what their mom did to them. They need to hash it out or forgive her or scream at her or whatever. But everyone pretending there's not this giant mom-size hole in their lives is getting a little ridiculous."

Patrick stared at her, then tipped his head back and laughed. "Right, and where will you be during World War Three?"

"Behind locked doors in Albany," she said with a smile.

Patrick set down his hammer, pushing himself up with much groaning and creaking knees. "You know," he said, "there are other holes in Gabe's life. Watching the two of you pretend that you don't still feel things for each other has been pretty ridiculous."

"Well—" she felt a blush ignite in her neck "—obviously we've stopped pretending."

"I'm not talking about sex." Patrick helped her to her feet and patted her shoulder. "I'm talking about the love that's running you two ragged."

Emotion surfaced and bobbed in her throat and she busied herself stacking the lightweight frames and supplies along the west window. "It's too hard," she said. "It's too hard to go back."

Patrick's eyes were liquid with compassion. Suddenly, she saw everything he hid behind his smiles and teasing. He was a man with a broken heart, living with one eye on the past.

"That's what I said years ago when my wife wanted to come home," he said, brushing his hands clean of sawdust and memories, "and I've never regretted anything more."

Patrick's words haunted Alice as she grabbed her flashlight and fleece jacket and headed back to her cabin. The heavy shadow of the Catskills made an already dark night even darker and not even the glimmer of a star broke up the ebony velvet of the sky. The moon was hidden behind trees and clouds.

Without the flashlight, Alice literally could not see her hand in front of her face.

She tripped over a tree root and barely caught herself before landing on her stomach in the dirt.

Such a difference from her illuminated and neon existence in the city and stranger still that she didn't miss that life, her car or her house. She did miss Felix, but really that was all.

Which didn't bode well for her return to it.

Her flashlight illuminated the front of her cottage, the closed door, the chair she'd placed on the small stoop.

Gabe sitting in that chair.

She stumbled again, her thumb hitting the button on the flashlight and the slice of light it provided vanished.

The night breathed.

"Gabe?" she whispered. He didn't answer but she heard the scuff of his shoe against the concrete, could feel him a few feet away. "What are you doing here?"

"Thinking."

Her heart tripped, and her skin, forgotten and cold, sang while it flooded with heat. Her eyes adjusted to the shadows and her body sensed his in the darkness.

"And?" she whispered, taking the small step up to stand near him.

"And I'm done thinking."

13

He reached out of the black night and folded her into his arms. His lips, despite the dark, unerringly found hers and all the confused desire between them fused into something new, different.

Dangerous.

She dropped the flashlight and wrapped her arms around him, tugged at the blond curls at the back of his neck and did all she could to climb into his skin.

He peeled the fleece from her shoulders and where the cool air should have chilled her he warmed her, lighting fires under her flesh. He cupped her shoulders, laced his fingers through her hair, kissed her neck. Her ear. Her lips again.

She groaned, pulling him closer, tighter. And he picked her up, her feet dangling over the ground, and spun her so her back hit the outside wall of the cottage.

"I've dreamed of this for so long," he muttered, yanking at the hem of her shirt and sliding his hand along her spine, up to her neck, then he held her still, immobilized as he devoured her mouth.

"Me, too." She sighed when he released her. She didn't bother with his shirt. Years of celibacy, years of remembering this man and his particular brand of fire, the way he could make her loose and crazy with just a look, made her bold and she reached for his belt.

With her fingers clumsy, her brain fevered, memory saved her. There were no years between them. No fights.

Just this.

His buckle clanged open and she undid the zipper, sliding her hand in between warm cotton and hot flesh. He gasped, groaned and shoved her against the wall. His chest hard against her, his lips open on her neck.

He bit her. She squeezed him, then he laughed—the devil's laugh—and the fire in her belly, across her skin, buried in her sex blazed hotter.

The contention in their marriage had seeped into their bedroom and sex had become a game of control between them. By the end, neither one of them gave themselves freely.

"This," he murmured against her skin, his breath tickling her ear and lighting her up. "This was something we always got right." He yanked open the top of her pants, the button flying off into the night. And his fingers, rough and big and so familiar, brushed her skin, the curve of her belly, the scar of the emergency C-section, the damp curls between her legs.

She saw stars on a starless night. The world spun and fell apart and Alice held him to her as hard as she could.

∼

Gabe rolled his head to look at the open window that was letting in all the cold air. Alice's body, pressed naked against his on top of the covers, was covered in goose bumps.

I should get up and close that, he thought. *Or we should get under the covers. Something.*

But moving—any movement—required herculean effort. And it might make Alice move away and, frankly, nothing was quite worth that. Not yet. Even cold and pressed against him, he didn't want her to move.

They had a limited number of these moments and he planned on making them last as long as possible.

And he did not plan on examining those feelings any further.

"Hey." Her voice was a raspy croak and he smiled hearing it.

"Hey."

"It's cold."

"Yep."

He felt her swallow against his chest. She turned her head and her chin dug into his ribs. He knew she was looking at him. "Do you want to stay?"

He stared at the ceiling, at the pine wainscoting that had cost him a fortune but had made the cabins something truly special.

"Gabe?"

He was a careful man, he took calculated risks and he never—well, not since getting involved with her the first time—made a move without weighing the costs.

What would I lose staying?

What would I gain leaving?

His head was too stupefied, too blurred by orgasm, to do

the math.

"I'm freezing," Alice said, her voice getting a little harder, her chin digging a little deeper. "So, if you're staying let's get under the blankets."

He lifted his head and smiled. "You always were good at the postcoital conversation."

She grinned and rolled away and he got infinitely colder.

Better go, his head said. *Better get out of here before things get worse. Messier. Because they always do with her.*

But she pulled down the duvet and in the shadows he could see the delicious curve of her breast, the swell of her hip and the scar bisecting her belly into top and bottom.

She would have been the mother of my children.

Thoughts of those babies, the boy and girl, who had been born too early, who were so small, the size of his palm, with their perfect eyelashes and paper-thin toenails. The babies he'd carried to Alice and they'd baptized with their tears before letting the nurses take away, while Alice screamed in her bed, had been banished long ago to places in his head he refused to visit. Doing so made living possible. Made recovering and getting on with his life easier.

But what was the cost? The rogue thought surfaced, from places unknown. *What was the cost of doing that?*

"Gabe?" she whispered, her hand fluttering awkwardly over that scar. "What's—"

He sat up, leaned forward, wrapped one arm around her thin yet strong back and pressed his lips to that scar, felt the small ridge under his tongue.

She gasped, dropped the blanket and put her hands in his hair, hugging his head to her belly.

He jerked the blankets down and pulled her into the warm envelope of the bed, his lips traveling from belly to breast, his tiredness forgotten, his reasons for leaving vanished.

"Gabe? What's—"

"No talking," he said, taking refuge in the sex they shared, like he always had. He wrapped his hands around her wrists, holding them against the bed and loved her the only way left to him.

"I've got a lot of work to do," Gabe said the following Saturday while he and Alice waited for her parents to arrive. "Really, there's the gutter situation on cabin five and I really should return Mrs. Crimpson's e-mail about the—"

"I told you," Alice interrupted with a laugh. Gabe's insecurity was actually pretty endearing right now, drunk as she was on sex and coffee. "You don't have to be here when my parents arrive. I can show them around myself and we don't need you for the meeting about what stations they'll staff at the wedding reception."

"I know." But he didn't leave.

"So, go ahead and get your work done." She bumped his hip with hers.

She was torn, as she had been for the week since Gabe had appeared up on her porch in the dark. Her heart sang some kind of crazy tune these days.

Nonstop.

While she taught Cameron how to ice a wedding cake, while she revised the menu every week, while she and Patrick worked on the wedding decorations. While she and Gabe made love. While they ate, while they worked side by side, while they debated East Coast cuisine versus West Coast. While they lay in bed, silent, curled around each other.

While she knew it was all going to end after the Crimpson wedding.

But her heart, stupidly, kept right on singing.

"You don't want to look like a coward?" she asked.

"I'm not a coward and—" he crossed his arms over his chest "—I'm not scared of your dad."

She laughed because her father was a scary man. A giant in their industry and a physical bear of a guy. Ten years ago, when she and Gabe had told him they were getting married and having a baby, her dad had taken Gabe outside for a little chat. Gabe had returned white-faced and calling him sir.

This would be the first time Gabe had seen them since the divorce.

"They won't blame you, Gabe," she said. "My parents understand better than most how hard I can be on a relationship."

Gabe slid an arm around her waist and pressed a kiss on her forehead.

But didn't say a word.

Alice wasn't stupid. So she kept her mouth shut but wished fervently that the Crimpsons would push the wedding back a few months. A year perhaps. Just until she and Gabe finished this long goodbye.

At the sight of her parents' old Volvo chugging up the gravel driveway Gabe dropped his arm and stepped away as if she were on fire.

But not fast enough for her dad. Michael saw the embrace through the driver's-side window and scowled.

"Hi, honey!" Her mom, Janice, a tiny elfish woman with

hands of steel from years of kneading homemade dough, leaped from the passenger's-side and jogged around the car to fold Alice in a hard hug. "Oh, look at you, sweetie. You look so good." Janice pulled back and cupped Alice's face in her hands. "A little lipstick wouldn't kill you," she whispered.

"Good to see you too, Mom." Alice laughed, accustomed to her mother.

"Quite a place you've got here," Michael said, stepping out of the car and standing to tower over Gabe. Dad had a beard and a belly and at least five inches on Gabe's six-foot frame.

"Thank you, sir." Gabe said, like a school-kid.

Michael's lip curled. "I told you ten years ago to call me Mike," he said and held out a giant paw for Gabe to shake. "Offer still stands."

Gabe sighed and shook his hand.

"Would you like a tour?" Gabe asked.

"We'd love one," Janice said and stepped over to kiss Gabe's cheek. "It's good to see you again."

Alice could tell he was surprised by their affection, surprised and moved. But it probably wouldn't last if her folks knew about this new relationship between them. So, Alice stepped in before her mom started asking questions and grabbed her dad's arm.

"Let's start with the kitchen," she said, pulling them into movement. "Cameron is my assistant, Dad. And I'm warning you, he's a kid, so go out of your way to be nice."

"Am I that scary?" he asked.

"Yes," Gabe answered from behind them and everyone laughed.

An hour later Alice and Janice walked arm in arm toward the gazebo, while her dad and Gabe unloaded the half-barrel barbecue from the back of the Volvo.

"So?" Janice asked. "It looks like things are going well."

Alice nodded but did not meet her mother's eyes.

"When is your contract up?"

"Three weeks."

"Have you found a replacement?"

She'd been ignoring that little issue. "Not yet. I've put out some feelers."

They stepped into the gazebo and Alice let go of her mom to go watch the Hudson flow by, wishing the questions her mother was bound to ask, had been asking with her eyes since setting foot on the property, would flow on by, too.

"Why are you lying, Alice?"

And no such luck.

"I've just been busy." Alice held her breath to see if her mom would accept that lame answer.

"What are you doing, sweetie?" Janice asked, sliding an arm over Alice's shoulders. She didn't have to clarify Alice knew what her mother meant. *What are you doing with Gabe? What are you doing with your life?*

"I don't know, Mom." She sighed. "I know it's a bad idea, but if you could see how different Gabe is right now. How different both of us are—"

"I'd see how it's okay for you to be involved with your ex-husband again?"

"You'd see how it's impossible not to be involved with him again."

"Just be careful. Find a replacement so that when things go bad—"

"Maybe they won't go bad," she whispered her stupid wish, words she only sighed against Gabe's chest in the dead of night with his sleeping breath in her ear.

"Oh, Alice." Janice pressed her lips to Alice's head and Alice closed her eyes. Her mom didn't need to say anything else; the words unsaid, blew through her, right into her foolish heart.

Things always went bad with Gabe.

Michael helped Alice with dinner, working the grill and putting a twist on her filet that earned raves out in the dining room.

"You want to replace me when my contract here is over?" she asked over the mouth of her water bottle when the last dessert had been plated and served and the dishwasher chugged away in the background.

Dad tipped back his head and laughed, swirling the red wine in his glass, before draining it. "Your mother would kill me."

She watched him swallow and waited for the demons to stir, but they remained silent, unmoved by the fruity noir her dad drank.

"I'm retired so she can have me paint the house and work in her garden," he said. He poured more wine into his glass and gestured with the bottle toward her.

"No, thanks," she said.

"That kid you got working here—"

"Cameron?" She smiled, remembering how Cameron had taken one look at her dad and all but ran from the room.

"He's got talent," Dad said. "Real talent."

"I think so, too. He's a good kid."

"Things working out for him at that group home?"

"Seem to be. He's only been there a week."

"Reminds me of Max."

"He reminds all of us of Max."

Gabe and Janice came in from the dining room laughing about something, but when Gabe saw the wine bottle, his laughter faded. His eyes darted to her, and when she lifted her bottle of water, he physically relaxed.

She wasn't offended, oddly. She understood the situation from his perspective now that she was sober and was grateful that he'd taken a risk on the wreck she'd been.

"You ready, sweetheart?" Janice asked, taking the wineglass from her husband's hand. "We need to get on the road now, if I'm driving."

"Oh, you're driving," Dad said.

"You can stay here," Gabe offered for the tenth time. "We've got lots of room."

"No, we need to head home," Janice said and the four of them walked out the kitchen door into the cool moonlight.

Alice longed to wrap her arm around Gabe's waist as they watched her folks get into the Volvo, her father fumbling with the seat controls so he could actually sit in the passenger's seat without eating his knees. Mom rolled her eyes and turned on the engine, the headlights taking slices out of the night. When the car turned and headed up the road, Gabe, as if he could read her mind, slid his arms around her shoulders, pulling her back against his chest.

"Your dad wants to kill me," he muttered into her hair.

"No, he doesn't," she said, resting her bottom in the cradle of his hips.

"He's always wanted to kill me. But your mom sure did go out of her way with Max."

"I thought she was going to give him a haircut there for a minute."

"Well, the guy could use it. He looks like he's been living in the bush."

They stood, loosely embracing, watching the taillights fade into the ebony dark.

"Is Max okay?" she asked.

"He's better than he was."

"What happened to him?"

"After he was shot in the line of duty and got out of the hospital, he quit the force and came out here. Dad and I have tried to talk about it but he insists he's fine."

"He's not," Alice said. She tilted her head back and kissed his cheek. "It never occurred to you to push him a little harder? Try a little more?"

"Good God, no. He'd probably shoot me if I tried." Gabe pressed kisses along her neck, slowly making his way to that spot on her collarbone that turned her to jelly.

"You know what I'd like to talk about?" he asked.

She laughed, pressing her back against him not as playfully this time. "I can imagine."

"You weren't drinking tonight," he said. He rested his lips against her neck and the kisses stopped.

She shook her head, plucking at his fingers where they clasped her belly.

"Is it hard?" he murmured.

"Not drinking?"

He nodded against her neck.

"No," she said truthfully, surprised that she hadn't even

been thinking about it. "I'm too busy, too preoccupied, too —" She stopped, caution suddenly making an appearance. She had been about to say happy, but that felt like some kind of declaration and that would spoil what was between them, scare him off like a deer on the side of the road.

This was supposed to be goodbye. They'd agreed on that.

"Good," he said and went back to kissing her neck. He stepped forward, pushing her with his body away from the lodge toward her cabin, which had, over the past week, become their cabin.

"I deserve a reward or something," she said. "Oh," he chuckled against her skin, sending goose bumps along her body. "I'll reward you."

14

"So?" Patrick asked, watching his son ignore him, pretending to focus on the men unloading the tables, chairs, dishes and linens they were renting for the wedding in two weeks. The sun had set and the men hustled to get the van unloaded before it became full dark.

"So what?" Gabe asked. "We're putting it in the gazebo, guys," he said to the men taking the tables out of the truck. They grunted and crossed the lawn toward the shelter.

"I hope Max got enough tarps," Gabe said, as if that was what they were discussing.

"Gabe," Patrick slapped a hand on his son's shoulder, wanting to shake him until he saw sense. "You're avoiding the issue."

"What issue?" Max asked, approaching them from the kitchen door.

"I don't know. Dad's got issues," Gabe told his brother, and Patrick looked heavenward for patience.

"Alice!" Patrick cried. "Alice is the issue. And what you've been doing in her cabin every night."

Gabe and Max shared a wry look.

"If I have to explain it to you..." Gabe said.

"Don't be smart with me, kid." Patrick growled in frustration. "I'm still your dad." Gabe's smart-ass grin faded. "You're headed for trouble and pretending like nothing is going on."

"Nothing is going on," Gabe said. "Thanks, guys." He shook the hands of the movers, and Patrick and his two boys watched the truck drive off. Gabe bent to pick up one of the boxes of linens, but Patrick, tired of this silence they maintained, this fear they were all cursed with, grabbed Gabe's arm and turned him to face him.

"Talk to me, son. Don't pretend like this is no big deal."

Gabe sighed. "Dad, it's...temporary. It's what's happening right now."

"What about after the wedding? When she's supposed to go?"

Gabe betrayed himself by looking at his hand for a split second and Patrick wanted to rejoice. *He is human after all.* "Then she goes home," he murmured. "This isn't a second chance."

"Why?" Max asked. "I mean, why isn't it?"

"You, too?" Gabe asked, shooting his brother a killing look. "I didn't know you two were so interested in my love life."

"You love her," Max said and Patrick nodded. "She loves you, it's so obvious Cameron asked me about it."

"That doesn't change anything," Gabe said.

Why am I protecting them? Patrick wondered. *What's the damn point?*

"Because you're a coward," Max said.

"Oh!" Gabe hooted. "And you're so brave? Why the hell are you here, Max?"

"Not what we're talking about, Gabe."

"No, God forbid we talk about what's wrong with you. We should just let you go wild in the woods and never ask what happened last year."

Yes! This was good. This was healthy, this is what real families did, they talked about things. They hammered out the hard stuff. He and his boys didn't need to be afraid of this, they could do it. Talk like men.

"Is it because you can't have kids with her?" Max asked. "There are other ways to create a family."

Gabe's fists clenched and Patrick watched his sons start to square off as though they were sixteen again. He didn't get in the way.

"You're ruining this second chance you've been given."

"What do you know about second chances?" Gabe asked. "Or family for that matter. You fight and fight and fight until there's no one left in the room."

Okay, maybe they were going a bit too far.

"Boys—" He held up his hands between them, but they shouldered him out of the way.

"I know I'd kill for a second chance with a woman like Alice. And you're throwing her away like you don't care."

Patrick's heart spasmed and ached for Max, his young son with the hidden wounds.

"Maybe I don't care! Maybe she doesn't. Maybe this is none of your damn business."

Gabe was in Max's face, a breath away from shoving him and Max, who loved a good knockdown, drag-out fight, stepped back, put his hands up.

"You're right," Max conceded and headed out toward the forest and whatever waited for him in the dark.

Patrick let out the breath he'd been holding. In the end the Mitchell way always won out. Avoid. Don't talk. Run.

Patrick saw what he'd done here, how the way he'd lied

to his sons, waited too long to tell them that their mother had left and then, in an effort to make the wounds heal faster, he'd pretended she'd never been there at all. Now both of his sons were doing it. Pretending they didn't even hear the drumbeat coming ever closer.

Gabe rubbed his hands over his face. "We're saying goodbye," he murmured. "That's all, it's what we agreed. We're ending our marriage the right way."

"By pretending it didn't end?" Patrick was seeing him with new eyes.

"No," Gabe said, cold steel in his blue eyes, "I will never forget that it ended."

"Is it because she can't have children?" Patrick asked. "You could adopt."

"When I brought it up before—" Gabe shook his head. "You should have seen her. It was like she couldn't stop crying. And then she couldn't stop screaming at me."

"But you're older. Wiser."

"We're just not meant to be together long-term. Let it go, Dad. There's too much between us to make it work."

"Like it would work better with someone you don't feel as much for?"

"Maybe."

Patrick stared at him slack jawed. "Your mom really did a number on you, didn't she?"

"I don't even think about her, Dad. I stopped years ago. She had nothing to do with this."

It broke Patrick's heart that his son couldn't see the truth of what he was doing—pushing away a good woman before he got hurt again. It was the same thing he'd done when Iris had asked to come home. He'd eliminated every chance that they might work, on the off chance they wouldn't. It was even worse that his wife wasn't here to see what she'd done to her boys with her middle-of-the-night abandonment of them.

She should see this, he thought, fuming.

Gabe bent to grab a box, ending the conversation, and Patrick, muttering under his breath, bent to help him.

"Gabe?" Alice said and both men looked up as if there'd been a gunshot. Patrick tried to discern whether she'd heard his son's callous words, but it was too dark, the light coming out from the kitchen door behind her too bright.

She doesn't deserve this, Patrick decided. Not Alice and not Iris. They didn't deserve to be so ignored, no matter what happened.

"Come in," she said, her voice merry and full of secrets. If she'd heard, she didn't reveal it. "I have something to show you."

$\sim$

Gabe's skin crawled. It crawled and itched, his muscles twitched, his brain hurt. The question he asked himself every day, every moment, dogged his footsteps as he walked into the dining room.

What am I doing?

The promise he made every night walking to her cottage, his blood on fire for her. The promise he made every night, when she curled up next to him echoed his question.

This will be the last time.

The dining room was dark, the last of the fading light making shadows across the ceiling and floor. There were things hanging from the rafters and he realized Alice had finished the decorations.

"Close your eyes." Her voice came out of the darkness like the loving hand of the wife she'd been.

Sad and torn and worried about the future, he did as she asked.

He heard the flip of a switch and light bloomed behind his eyelids.

"Open them," she said and his eyes opened to a surreal water landscape. The silks covered the ceiling, blowing slightly with the ceiling fans she'd turned on, undulated like waves across the wooden beams. Long cords hung down among the silks and ended in old round Christmas-tree lights of the clear variety, and among the waves and the half dark, they looked like bubbles all across the ceiling, at different lengths and different intensities.

He took a slow turn, admiring her vision, her work, and wishing all the while that things were different.

"I could put up a few anchors if you think it would be better," she said and he realized she'd taken his silence for disapproval.

"Not on your life," he said, he couldn't look at her, not yet. "It's amazing, Alice. Really beautiful."

She sidled up to him, wrapping her arm around his waist and he felt so guilty for his words out in the yard, his callous, deliberate misunderstanding of what was between them that he stepped away, making it seem as though he wasn't quite done looking around.

"I'm sort of hoping she wants a disco ball," Alice said. "Then it would really look like we were underwater."

Gabe laughed and worked at getting himself back in check. Back on point. He watched her from the corner of his eye as she stared at her work, a satisfied smile on her lips. So beautiful, so different from the woman he'd hired.

But, history repeats itself. And their's was bloody and painful. He didn't need any more lessons in how incompatible they were when the going got tough. In these times— easy and happy and hard at work—they could survive, help each other. But any moment things could go wrong and then the truth of their marriage would win out.

Right?

He couldn't gamble that it would be different. There was too much at stake.

Gabe felt as if his skin were falling off in great strips, his back, his chest were naked, his heart pounded under muscle and bone, flinching from the cold air.

I want a family. I want children. Grandchildren. I want to watch my dad teaching my kids how to sand wood, and watch Max showing them the differences between red and white oak. I want babies and the terrible twos and driving lessons and failed science tests. I want it all.

And I can't have it with her.

"I can take it down in the morning," she said. "I just wanted to make sure it would all work before it's too late." She pulled her ever-present notebook out of her back pocket. "We've got one week before the family arrives and two weeks before everyone else arrives and we start the rehearsal dinner and wedding activities."

It was the time line, the hourglass running out of sand, and he felt as if he were in a race. Love her, love her as much as he could before she left. Touch her and kiss her and hold her close because in two weeks it was over.

"My folks will come in that last week and we'll get all our prep done. We can—"

He knocked the notebook out of her hands and hauled

her into his arms. The pins fell out of her hair at the rough touch of his fingers and her arms were hard and fast around him as if she, too, understood it was all coming to an end.

She swung up in his arms as if pushed by some force and he was led out of the lodge by something outside of himself. Their clothes fell off and they never stopped kissing.

He felt his heart gathering itself, beating faster toward something. Something dark and stupid and foolish.

This is the last time.

The thought pounded in his brain as he kissed her throat.

I can't do this anymore.

The truth screamed through his blood as his hands cupped her hips, her waist, the light swell of her breast.

Gotta slow down, he realized. Everything felt too out of control—her breath against his chest, her hands on his body, the growling sighs from the back of her throat. It all felt as though it spun too fast toward oblivion.

Slow down.

He lowered her back onto the bed. Pushed away her hands when she reached for him. He crawled down her body, ignoring her efforts to pull him up.

"Ask me," he said, seeking distance in these games of control and contrition that they excelled at. He kissed her belly, blew cool air across the damp curls at the apex of her thighs.

"No, Gabe."

He chuckled, glad she played her part with such skill.

"Ask me, Alice." He kissed her thigh, traced that sweet tendon at her hip with his tongue. "You're going to have to ask me."

Her hands, strong and cool, framed his face and forced

him to look up at her, her black eyes gleaming in the dark. "Love me, Gabe. Like it was in the beginning."

His heart exploded in painful joyous memories of two people in love, looking at each other while they kissed, while they orgasmed, two people so naked in their need for each other that there was no need for games.

Two people, unwounded, free from scars, with no idea that loving would be so painful.

He shook his head, dislodging her hands. He couldn't do it.

"Please," she sighed. "Please, Gabe. No games. Not tonight."

He couldn't move, torn between staying and leaving. Loving her his way or hers.

In his silence and inaction, she took over.

"Shh," she whispered, sitting up. "It's okay, Gabe. It's just me." She brushed the hair back from his face and smiled crookedly into his eyes. "Just us." She kissed him, pushed him onto his back and he allowed it to happen even though he knew where it would end—the destruction of the barriers he kept around himself, the removal of the cushions he kept on the sharp corners of things that could hurt him all over again.

I love her.

I love her and I can't be with her.

"Just this," she breathed into his ear, peppering his face with small kisses, his lips with tiny bites. She held his hand, put it to her face, looked into his eyes.

And loved him.

∾

Alice turned her head, stared out the window at the sky turning gray and pink, and fought back tears when she heard Gabe stand up and start to get dressed.

She wished she could be more surprised, summon up some stunned outrage that he could love her and leave her this way.

But she wasn't surprised.

She'd known the moment was coming when he stared, heartbroken, into her face as they made love. As he'd kissed her as if it were the last time.

Grief and anger warred in her. Maybe if she hadn't pushed the issue, forced him to truly make love to her. Maybe if she'd waited. Maybe if he wasn't such a coward.

There were so many maybes.

"I need to go," he said.

"You haven't slept," she said, as if he'd say, "You're right, scoot over," and climb back in with her rather than do what she knew he was about to do.

"Too much work to do." He shot her a grin over his shoulder that struck sorrow in her heart. The man she'd made love to, looked in the eye while he came, had left the building, and this Gabe, this slick, uncaring man, was about to end it all. "I'm not sure how much time we're going to have in the next little while."

She sat up.

"So, if we can't—"

"Turn around, Gabe." Her voice was iron again and he stiffened, hesitated, but finally turned to face her. She'd known this moment was coming since this affair started, but when she'd overheard Gabe and Patrick talking tonight, she knew it was coming sooner, rather than later.

Sooner as in right now.

"I would adopt," she murmured. She was older, wiser, more adept at reality, at understanding that not being able to have children did not make her less of a person. Adoption sounded like a good idea, if it meant she could build a family with this man.

He didn't say anything for a moment, he simply gaped at her, thunderstruck, and she rushed to fill the silence. "I heard you talking to your dad. And you're right. This is supposed to be goodbye, but—" She swallowed, looked down quickly at the edge of the sheet she pleated in her hands. "But I don't want it to be."

"We don't work," he whispered. "Remember?"

She shook her head. "Not as well as I used to." She tried to smile, but in the end she just stared at him, willing him to reveal himself to her—his true self, not this man of obstinance and fear. "You can't tell me you haven't been thinking about it."

"About what exactly?" he asked.

"About trying again. About second chances." She took a deep breath. "About regrets."

"Sure," he said honestly. "But I've also been thinking about the fights. And the tears. And how we went out of our way to hurt each other. I've been thinking about how you said you were tired of being disappointed in me. That I wasn't the man you thought I was."

Echoes from their fights and those words, meant to hurt, had scarred him. Three months ago she would have been delighted to know she'd managed to affect him in some way. But now, watching him gather himself to leave her again, she wished desperately that she'd never said such hurtful things.

"But it feels so different right now, doesn't it?" she asked.

"If we could just sit down and talk about how we feel about the miscarriages—"

He jerked on his shirt and shoved his feet into his boots, muttering under his breath. She'd pushed him too far.

I should have kept my mouth shut. This was too much. Too fast. He can't handle all this.

"What are you doing?" She grabbed his arms, fighting for her life. "Why are you running?"

"I'm not running, I just have to go."

"What did I say?" she asked, feeling panicked and hurt.

"We can't get over the past—"

"Right," she cried. "Not if you don't talk about it. Sit down and we can talk—"

"I don't want to talk about anything!" he yelled, pulling her hands off his arms. "This isn't a second chance. It's goodbye. Like we agreed."

He looked at her with frozen eyes, his face glacial. His heart unreachable. She sat back on the bed, cold. Alone.

"Go," she said. "Get out."

He left without another word.

He went to his room, stripping off the clothes that smelled of her. Of sex. Of two people doing stupid things, and fell exhausted across his bed. His eyes shut briefly and he saw those babies. His children. He felt them in his hands, their still chests and cold skin.

He gouged his fists in his eyes, trying to shove those images away. Push them out of his head.

He didn't want to talk about them. Think about them.

And being with Alice again, talking about adoption. Regrets. Jesus, how much did a guy have to take?

Everything hurt—his body, his head. He rubbed at his chest, where it felt as if something sat on him, crushing him. He struggled for breath.

It hurt. It hurt worse than the first time, when he'd been so anxious to leave. This time he could have stayed, could have climbed back into bed with her and talked about adoption.

He sat up.

It was best this way. They'd be busy, then she'd be gone and life could return to some sort of equilibrium. He could concentrate on those things that were important to him now. He couldn't go back to those failed dreams, sifting through the ashes of what they'd once had to see what could be reused. It would only be a matter of time before the fighting started again, over something else.

He put his hands to his eyes again, feeling them burn beneath his fingers. But a baby...

He shook his head and stood. It was dawn and since there was no way he could sleep now he figured he might as well get to work.

Patrick sat back from the table and studied the objects of his downfall. His hemlock and poison asp. They looked like mere pen and paper, lined up square against each other waiting for him to set in motion what could be the worst mistake he'd ever made.

He took another sip of the fine scotch that seemed suited

to this moment of big decisions and strong emotion. A swig for the soon to be executed.

He tilted his head back, felt the burn of the fine liquor in his belly and allowed himself to wonder for the very last time if this was the right thing to do.

She'd been sick in some way. He knew that. There was something dark that lived in her that he couldn't touch all those years ago. A demon that had run him ragged and he was inviting it back.

He sucked back the last of the booze, picked up the pen and scrawled:

Come. We'll be waiting.

He threw down the pen, folded the paper, crammed it into an envelope, not stopping when he tore the paper and crinkled the envelope. He licked the seal, put the return address in the corner so she'd know where he was, so she wouldn't have to go through their lawyer. He called his lawyer and left a message to have someone come and pick up the letter first thing in the morning.

"Done," he said, his heart thundering around his chest like some jackrabbit. For good or bad it was done.

15

Alice made every effort to take this second breakup in stride. To convince herself she'd been wrong, that Gabe, with his fear of intimacy and abandonment issues, was right.

This was better. Really. It was better being alone in that bed, for the past three nights.

But these few weeks with him back in her arms had scattered the previous five years like birds, as if they'd never happened. His empty side of the bed was a gaping wound all over again.

And despite her efforts, she wasn't convinced that it was better feeling as if she couldn't breathe every time they were in the same room. Or that it was better waiting with pounding heart and cold hands for him to enter the room so she could pretend he wasn't there.

"Hey," Cameron said over her shoulder, while she worked mindlessly on a bowl of egg whites. "Is that supposed to be meringue?"

She looked down to see egg whites the consistency of library glue around her fork.

Disgusted with herself, she threw the bowl down on the counter.

"You...okay?" Cameron asked just as Gabe walked in the door, crossed the corner of the kitchen as if no one was there and slammed the door of his office shut.

She and Cameron watched and flinched at the noise.

"What's with him?" Cameron asked and Alice, sad and sick of being sad, swore. Like a sailor. A sailor who only knew swearwords.

Cameron's eyebrows skyrocketed.

"Sorry," she muttered. "I'm just...frustrated."

"Is it the wedding?" he asked. "I mean, because we're behind on the prep or something?" He was so worried that he might have something to do with what was wrong that her heart went out to him.

Six weeks ago this faith, this pressure he put on her—to be at least a participant in this relationship, to give him the smallest crumbs of affection and loyalty—would have sent her running for the door. Right now she wanted to hug him. She wanted to promise that nothing else would hurt him.

As much as that was a lie.

"Not at all," she assured him. "We're ahead of schedule. The families arrive in five days and all we need to do is figure out what to serve them the first night they're here."

He nodded, fidgeting slightly with the tie on his apron.

"Did you have an idea?"

"Well, I've been looking at your books, you know..." He pointed to her shelf of cookbooks and grabbed her old family one, grease spattered and dirty. "I like this one." He flipped to the grilled rabbit stuffed with parma ham and herbs.

"Rabbit?"

"Max said it tastes like chicken. We could serve it with this." He turned the page to the delicious springtime risotto.

"Yeah, but rabbit?"

"It's probably a dumb idea." Defeated, he shut the book and started to put it back on the shelf.

It might very well be the least appropriate meal to greet them with, she thought. Time intensive and hard work for just the two of them. Heavy and oddly paired and—

What did it matter? she wondered suddenly. In the long run the Crimpsons would forget that meal, but Cameron would never forget the chance to put this meal together.

Sometimes the greater good, the real payoff was hidden behind compromise, lost among the wrong priorities.

Alice braced herself against the counter as the new reality of her life settled in around her.

Look at me, she thought. *Look at me with this boy. Before I came here I never would have sacrificed something for his feelings. Oh my God, three nights ago I told Gabe I would adopt.*

She put her hand to her forehead. When did this happen?

She'd been focused so hard on Gabe, on making them work, that she'd missed what was truly important. She was over the past. Well, maybe not over, but getting over it. Those children didn't haunt her. Adoption sounded like a good idea, it still did, with or without Gabe. She wanted a family and was ready to get it, find it. Beg, borrow and steal it.

She was sober. Working.

She was happy.

"Rabbit it is." She nodded, grabbing the cookbook. "I'm going to need you to call our butcher and get this set up for fourteen people. And we're going to need a lesson in risotto."

He looked at her, slack jawed. "You sure? I mean, I could screw it up—"

"Yep, but that's how you learn."

Cameron took a deep breath and took the book. "Can I work the grill?"

"Not on your life."

Gabe opened the office door and stormed out into the dining room, again pretending the two of them weren't there.

She saw him with new eyes, and while it hurt, while her whole body hurt from the force with which she wished they could work it out, she knew they wouldn't, not until he got where she was.

Pretending the past never happened didn't make it go away. His mother leaving, the babies dying, the marriage falling apart, they all ate away at him and he'd never let anyone close again until he figured it out.

She watched him go and felt her heart strain after him.

"You know what my dad taught me?" Cameron asked.

"I can't even imagine," she said, trying to pull herself together.

"You can't make someone love you," he said. His eyes were far too old, too all seeing for a boy his age. "I tried and tried," he said, and shrugged.

I love Gabe, she realized. *I always will, but there's nothing more I can do.*

Alice sighed and before Cameron could flinch or run away she hugged him. Hard.

"I'm so glad you're here," she said. "I'm glad I met you."

Awkwardly, carefully, Cameron hugged her back.

≈

Alice loaded the herbs and vegetables needed for Cameron's meal into the backseat of her car. She'd come here, to Athens Organics, on a two-part mission. Get veggies. Apologize to Daphne.

But it wasn't as easy as she'd thought it would be.

It wasn't as though there was a Hallmark card dedicated to this kind of thing.

Sorry my ex-husband dumped you to date me, only to dump me, too.

Too bad we fell for the same intimacy-phobe, wanna chat?

"How are the wedding plans going?" Daphne asked, brushing the dirt off her hands onto the seat of her jeans.

"So far so good." Alice shielded her eyes with her hand so she could better see Daphne, gauging if the woman was furious or not. So far it didn't seem so. "But that usually means we're missing something."

"Wedding?" Helen asked, looking up from what seemed to be an intricate sketch she was drawing in the dirt with her shoe. "What wedding?"

"At the inn," Alice said, smiling at the little girl. Maybe coming here had a three-part goal. Apologize. Get food. Test acceptance of the past, by standing in the company of this little girl who would be the age of her own daughter.

And so far, judging by how badly she wanted to straighten Helen's ponytail and squeeze her, she was doing okay.

"Can we go?" Helen asked her mom.

"Sorry, sweetie, but—"

"Of course," Alice interjected, surprising everyone, most of all herself. She had no business inviting people to the wedding. But she wasn't really going to let that stop her. She could handle the Fish-Stick Princess on behalf of this little girl.

"Are you sure that's okay?" Daphne asked.

"Why not," Alice said, tapping into this new attitude of hers. She felt breezy and fluid, expansive and loving. Toward everyone.

"I've never been to a wedding!" Helen cried. "Will we dance?"

"Absolutely!"

"Will there be flowers?"

"They're being delivered and planted right now."

"Mommy! Mommy! Can we go? Can we?" She grabbed her mother's hand and nearly knocked her off balance with her hopping and leaping.

"We can stop by," she said in a stern voice. "We can see how the inn looks and then we'll leave."

"We can dance?"

"One dance."

It was enough for Helen, who went spinning off into the backyard.

Daphne eyed her sideways, and Alice smiled. "It will be fine. There are other kids invited and I'll double-check with the bride."

"That's not what I'm worried about," Daphne said. "You're a different woman today than you were the last time I saw you. I take it things with you and Gabe worked out?"

Alice's heart spasmed and gushed hot blood, proving she wasn't as okay with their breakup as she wanted to pretend. She swallowed back the sudden pain and shook her head. "Nope," she said. "We crashed and burned, like we always do."

"So? What's with this happy version of the bitter chef?"

She smiled at the description and was glad the bitterness was gone.

"I realized I can't change him. He's got to do it himself. So, I took the energy I was throwing his way and used it to make myself happy."

"And it's working?"

"Most of the time." Alice was again blindsided by a swell of feelings for Gabe. "I wish things were different, but—" She took a shaky breath and Daphne touched her arm, forestalling her.

"Good for you."

Alice laughed. "Well, we'll see about that. But I'm serious about you two coming to the wedding. I swear, they won't even notice."

"Well." Daphne looked out after her daughter who was showing one of the farm employees a spectacular twirl. "I don't think I could keep her away." They both laughed and it felt so good to do it that Alice nearly wept.

Jeez, I'm emotional, she thought, and got into her car before she cried like a baby in front of Daphne.

Gabe was mad. He was mad at the landscapers who had showed up late and were taking their time planting the flowers around the property and managed to destroy the grass in front of cottage four.

But mostly he was mad at Max.

"Go away," he said for perhaps the twentieth time.

"Gabe, I'm telling you, we've got to talk about this."

"We already did." Gabe stepped away and bent to

reposition the orange, yellow and red daylilies that were going to be planted around the gazebo.

"Jesus, you're stubborn."

Gabe swung incredulous eyes up at his brother. "Hello, pot," he muttered.

"Dad is acting different. Something has happened."

"Dad has been acting different all spring. We figured it out—Mom contacted him. That's it."

"Yeah, but have you noticed that he stopped talking about her? And he's walking around whistling—"

"He realized we were right and that it's better to just leave it alone." He decided to go see how the flower beds around the entrance to the lodge were doing, hoping his brother would give up and head back to his cave in the woods, or wherever he'd been spending most of his time.

But Max grabbed him and the anger that was simmering in Gabe's bloodstream boiled over.

"What the hell is wrong with you?" Gabe snapped, knocking Max's hands loose. "Dad's better, he's not moping around like some teenager. Leave it alone."

Max blinked at him. "You're like one of those birds that keeps his head in the sand all the time. Don't you wonder why he's acting better? Do you think it just magically happened? And what about Alice? Why's she—"

Gabe took off again, he didn't want to listen to this. He didn't have to. It was his inn. "You're fired," he said. "Go bother someone else."

Max stepped out in front of him and Gabe, who knew he'd never win a fistfight with Max—hadn't since he was seven—decided he didn't care.

He punched his brother right in the face. Max staggered back and Gabe, his hand on fire and his anger only growing, stalked past him.

Max tackled him from behind. Gabe landed on the ground with an "*ufff!*" and possibly a cracked rib. Max rolled him over and sat on him, using his knees to hold Gabe's hands down.

"Dirty trick!" Gabe hollered, bucking up only to be shoved back down by his bigger former-cop brother.

"Yeah, well, you deserve it."

"Get the hell off me."

"No."

Gabe bucked and twisted and managed to get one solid punch to his brother's stomach, knocked him off balance and rolled over him, digging his elbows into Max's sides, rubbing his face in the dirt. But victory was short and soon Max had him pinned.

"Mom left on a Tuesday," he said and Gabe scrambled to get free, but Max grabbed his leg and pulled him back. "She kissed us good-night, remember? She sat on your bed and told us a joke about a penguin and a chicken."

"Shut up."

"We went downstairs that morning and we sat in our places and we waited for what seemed like hours—"

"Max, I'm serious." Something was cracking in his chest, that rib maybe. His stupid brother, of course, would break his ribs. He tried to rub away the pain. "You are so fired."

"We did that every morning for two weeks. You refused to go to school, remember? You made her pancakes every day and we watched them get cold on the table. Ring any bells in that stupid head?"

"No!"

"You stopped eating and I did whatever you did. Finally Dad begged you to eat something and you said you'd only eat if Mom came back and that's when he told us that she wasn't going to come back. You said 'Never?' And Dad nodded, crying his eyes out and I waited for you to cry. I waited, and I waited, and you just watched Dad, then finally you said, 'Good.'"

Gabe couldn't breathe, the earth wasn't at his back and he was flung into empty space, a free fall into nothing.

"You said *good*." Max shook his head, rolled away from Gabe but he still couldn't stand up. All his bones were broken. The dam shattered and the past swept him up and away. "I couldn't believe it. Dad tried to tell you not to be so angry but you wouldn't hear it. I've never seen you grieve for Mom. Ever."

Gabe lay on the grass and stared up at the sky, the memory as fresh as if she'd left him yesterday.

"I still feel that way," he whispered. "I know he wants us to see her, but—" he shook his head "—I can't."

Max flopped onto his back beside Gabe and neither of them mentioned how odd this was, two grown men lying on a lawn after trying to beat the hell out of each other.

"You know, I've tried and tried to think of why she would leave. Were we bad? Did Dad do something wrong? Was it another man?"

"I don't know. I remember she cried a lot."

"You do?" Gabe asked, stunned. "I don't remember that at all."

Max shrugged. "We were kids, who knows if it's real or not."

"What do you think?" Gabe asked Max. "Do you want to see her?"

Max shrugged. "I kind of want to yell at her. Tell her what she did to us and Dad." They were silent for a long time. "What happened with Alice?" Max asked.

Gabe felt that anger well up in him again. "Nothing." He stood and walked away, wiping the grass off his pants as

he went as if they were memories that clung so deter-
minedly.

"You never grieved for her, either," Max said. "Or those
babies."

"Shut up, Max."

"You know I'm right."

Gabe broke into a run toward the lodge.

He stepped into the kitchen from the dining room just as
Alice came in the back door, her arms filled with a box of
vegetables.

"Gabe!" Her brow knit with concern. "What happened to
your face?"

He touched the corner of his split and bloodied lip and
winced. "My brother," he said.

"What's wrong?" She slid the box onto the counter and
crossed her arms over her chest. The kitchen swirled with
tension, with everything they wanted to say and do. He
wanted to fold her into his arms, have her kiss away the pain
of his bruises and at the same time he wanted to bundle her
up and send her home. That dichotomy was tearing him
apart. Tearing apart the whole damn inn.

"Gabe." Her face softened. She knew what he was going
through and had the power to make it better. But he knew
what she wanted. She wanted to repeat the past, hash it out,
pull it into the present and go on from there.

"Do you have a replacement?" he asked, stone-faced and
angry, and she shut down in response.

Stop caring, he wanted to say. *Just give up on us. We're not
worth the pain.*

"I'm looking, Gabe," she said as calmly as she could.
"Tim Munez called me back yesterday but I've been too
busy to get in touch with him."

"Tim would be good."

She bit her lip and nodded, turning back to her vegetables. "I have work to do," she said.

He watched her take the box to the fridge and start putting away her produce. He knew he needed to apologize, he wasn't handling any of this well.

"Alice, I don't mean to be so—"

"I get it, Gabe," she interrupted, throwing spinach into the bottom drawer of the fridge. "Everything will be easier when I'm gone. For both of us."

"Something like that," he said and, with the die cast, he finally turned away, feeling worse than when he'd come in.

16

"It's beautiful, Gabe." Gloria Crimpson and her heavily pregnant daughter toured the grounds and Gabe listened to her with half an ear. "It's exactly as you promised."

"I'm glad you like it," he murmured. Gloria looked over her pink Chanel-clad shoulder at him. He smiled, trying to reassure her. Trying to get in the game. This was a big day for him and he felt as though he watched it all through a fog he couldn't get clear of.

"David's folks should get here tonight," Savanah said, so in love and so young that the prospect only brought joy to her, despite Gloria's pinched lips pinching farther. "I can't wait to show them the cabins. They are so amazing!"

Gabe wished he could snap out of this funk and revel in the success of everything. But the funk was stubborn and his brother walking around with a shiner and Alice suddenly being Mary Sunshine as if this weren't their last week of seeing each other, as if it didn't matter that she would be leaving soon, didn't help.

"Thank you," he said. "They turned out even better than I had thought, too."

"When do the decorations go up?" Savanah asked. "They looked so beautiful on the sketches."

"The night before," he answered.

"Your chef made them?" she asked and when he nodded she laughed. "That's a talented chef."

You don't know the half of it, he thought, wishing she were here instead of him right now. In the past few days dealing with these women she'd been taking the lead, possessing a sudden sweetness compared to his unabating sour attitude. He'd thought she was different during their brief rekindling —laughing, working hard, loving her work. But this new Alice—welcoming and open and gregarious—he had never seen her. Ever.

His attraction to her doubled and redoubled every time he saw her hug Cameron, or offer the delivery guys coffee and cinnamon rolls. Every time she teased his brother and dad as if they were her own.

She needed to leave. Soon.

"Not judging by last night's meal," Gloria, whose acidic voice, normally loaded to capacity with superiority and judgment, managed to sharpen just a bit more on.

"It was wonderful," Savanah insisted. "I've never had rabbit before."

"I should say not. You weren't raised in the hills."

Gloria kept up her pace across the grounds despite her high heels and narrow skirt. Gabe and Savanah lagged behind momentarily.

"You'll have to excuse my mom," she said, stroking the round mound of her belly. "She's not taking this pregnancy and small nonsociety wedding very well."

"I hadn't noticed." He tried to say it magnanimously but it came out coated in sarcasm.

"Ah." She swiped her long curtain of shiny blond hair over her shoulder like a woman in a shampoo ad. "Our unflappable host finally shows some cracks." She said it with a laugh so Gabe didn't jump to his own defense. He didn't have the energy.

"We tried to book three other small inns along the Hudson and after the second conversation with my mother all three of them backed out." The girl seemed to expect this reaction without any rancor and he found himself watching her, slightly astonished by the reality of the Fish-Stick Princess.

"But not you." She shook her head and whistled. "I resorted to pink swans and sushi boats and you still didn't crumble."

Gabe gaped at her. "You wanted us to back out of the contract?"

She smiled and patted Gabe's shoulder. "David and I always wanted to elope. This wedding is a compromise for my parents and I was trying my best to weasel out of it." She winced comically and Gabe felt some true affection for the surprising Savanah. "Not the most honorable thing, but I couldn't imagine my marriage, the creation of my family, taking place in front of seven hundred people I don't care about."

"I understand," Gabe said as they strolled. "It's a very personal thing. I hope having your wedding here won't seem like such a bad compromise."

"It won't be. This is so beautiful, I couldn't have even imagined it. I am so grateful you didn't get run off by those pink swans."

He laughed and patted her shoulder. "It takes more than

pink swans to chase me off," he said and swallowed.

"I'm glad."

"Savanah!" Gloria shouted from the newly planted rose garden. "What's the problem? Are you okay?"

"I'm fine, Mom." Savanah rolled her eyes and picked up her pace. "You know in the end it only proves something I've learned from my mother."

"What's that?" Gabe asked, matching her stride.

"That I can't control everything. Sometimes you have to embrace what the world puts in your way."

Gabe stopped for a moment, the world slightly tilted under his feet.

"Gabe?" Savanah placed a hand on his arm.

"Sorry." He smiled without much heart, wondering what other surprises were in store for him this week.

Alice sent out the last of the lamb loins, served with the cucumber riata and fresh tomatoes. Elizabeth, one of the waitstaff, opened the door to the dining room and the sound of laughter came flooding in. The bride's and groom's parents certainly got along, though Alice wasn't surprised. David Barister and his folks, when she'd met them today, seemed to be truly lovely people. Lovely enough to round off Gloria Crimpson's sharp edges.

Of course, the bottles of wine they were going through didn't hurt.

She tossed the pan in the sink and the gamy smell of cooked lamb and garlic punched her in the face. She staggered away and tried to breathe fresh air before she lost her dinner all over the kitchen.

Oh God, she thought, swallowing nausea and bile. *This place is getting to me. I need a vacation.*

The phone in Gabe's office rang.

"Cameron?" she said, and her apprentice looked up from the lemon torte he was setting out to serve at room temperature. "I'll be right back."

"Okay," he said. "I'm going to play with the grill," he joked.

Alice threw the towel from her shoulder at him and went to grab the phone on Gabe's desk by the third ring.

"Riverview Inn, this is Alice."

"Hey, Alice. It's Tim Munez."

"Tim!" The nausea in her stomach tightened into knots and she sat in Gabe's chair, trying to ignore the smell of him that wrapped around her like an embrace. "How are you?"

"Fantastic." Tim said and Alice smiled. He was an infectiously cheerful man. The two years they'd shared a kitchen in Albany had been two of the most fun years of her career. "Really good. How are things on that mountain?"

"Better every week, Tim." She nearly laughed at the lie.

"Well, the spread in *New York Magazine* made that place look like heaven on earth."

"It is, Tim. So, have you thought about coming to work here?"

"Yep, and I'd love to do it."

She sighed and melted into the chair, a thousand pounds lifted from her, while another thousand resettled on her shoulders.

This is it. I'm leaving. It's over.

"But—" Tim said and her muscles reseized.

"But what?"

"I can't come on the date you wanted. I need two more weeks. I'm training my replacement here and it's going a bit slower than planned."

Alice spun and looked at the calendar on the wall behind her and did some quick math. She could do it. She could stay an extra two weeks.

Her heart pounded. It was a curse and a blessing. She was torn right down the middle between wanting to be here and wanting to put this place in her rearview mirror.

"No problem, Tim. We'll see you at the end of June."

"Excellent. I can't wait."

Alice hung up and continued to study the calendar. The wedding weekend was the tenth, which would make Tim's arrival the twenty-fourth, and she would stick around two days and—

She blinked.

Today was the fifth.

Her period was two days late.

As if summoned, the nausea gurgled in her stomach and she raced to the bathroom to throw up.

Hope, fear and dread churned through Alice's brain, eating away at her nerves for the next three days. Every time she went to the bathroom she was sure she would see blood. Sure that her period was only delayed by stress and the fact that she had no appetite whatsoever.

But every time, there was no blood, and hope would replace dread. Then upon thinking about a baby, about miscarrying again, fear would replace hope and the vicious cycle would spin.

I should tell Gabe, she thought as she sugared flowers to place on the wedding cake. She took a purple pansy, dipped it in egg white and sugar and placed it on a wire rack to dry.

I should tell him.

But she didn't.

Another day went by and her period still didn't come. Guests began to arrive. Her parents came in the evenings and helped finish the prep work and it was all background noise, to the constant conversation she had in her head.

I should tell him.

There's no point in telling him if I don't know for sure. Why get him all worked up?

She never bought a pregnancy test—she put it off and put it off.

Another day went by.

Hope was unfettered, a giant bird loose in her body. She stopped drinking coffee.

"Are you kidding?" Max asked as he waited, cup in hand, for the coffee machine to stop brewing one early morning with the sky just beginning to lighten. "No coffee?"

"It's bad for you."

Max scowled at her. "You've lost it."

Find out! she thought. *Just find out for sure.*

But then there were problems with her decorations. In storage a panel of silk tore from its frame and she and Max spent hours repairing it.

"You all right?" he asked while she mended the silk that had torn and he hammered a new nail into the corner joint.

"I'm great." She smiled at him. "Why?"

"You seem a little juiced."

"Juiced?"

"Yeah, like you're on something. And I know it's not coffee."

"Right." She laughed. "I've managed to find the time to start a drug habit."

"I thought maybe it was Gabe. Maybe you fixed things."

Hope, that giant bird on the loose fell like a stone in her stomach. Reality crashed in around her and she couldn't laugh. Her face felt suddenly paralyzed.

I might be pregnant with Gabe's baby. Again. The nightmare might start all over. Again. She rubbed her forehead. What if she told him and he asked her to marry him, then she lost the baby? Again.

She swallowed back a sudden painful sob.

This was a horrific roller coaster she couldn't get off.

It was ludicrous that she could be pregnant after the years, money and procedures dedicated to getting this way. But it was like those women in that counseling group who, years after accepting their fates, ended up knocked up.

When you let go of the obsession, some of them said, laughing and flushed with their unbelievable luck, *it happens*.

Hormonal changes, that's why it happens, said the science-minded.

God, declared the religious.

She'd sat there and doubted all of them.

And yet here she was. Poised on this terrible precipice.

Do I want to try this again? Go through all of this again?

But, hope tried to say, what if she took it easy? What if she went on modified bed rest, and was really careful and Gabe could help her?

She shook her head, clearing hope's voice from her brain.

I don't even know for sure, she rationalized.

"Alice?" Max asked. He touched her shoulder and she flinched. "You all right?"

"Yeah." She sighed. "I—" She swallowed and felt the sudden burn of tears. "I'll be right back."

She stood and ran for the bathroom, feeling Max's suspicious gaze on her as she ran.

~

This is crazy, Gabe told himself. *You're crazy. The stress has finally eaten your brain and now you are standing outside your ex-wife's cottage like a stalker.*

Worse, this was his third night out here.

He felt as if the proverbial other shoe was poised above his head, waiting for him to relax so it could fall and crush him. Alice didn't look good these days and he wondered if she was drinking again. He told himself he was out here, watching her in her cabin to make sure she wasn't. But the truth was, this was the only place he could actually take full breaths of air.

Everything was going fine. The wedding was four days away and the details that he checked and rechecked obsessively so as to keep thoughts of Alice and his mother away seemed straightforward and taken care of.

So what the hell is wrong with me? Why am I here?

Because in his office, his stomach burned as if filled with acid. And in his room, his chest ached and he couldn't sleep.

He watched David and Savanah, day in and day out, young, in love, expecting their first baby, and missing Alice felt like an open wound.

It would be better when she was gone, when she wasn't

constantly there reminding him of things they would never have.

But then where will I go to breathe?

"Gabe?"

He whirled away from the cabin he'd been watching only to find Alice on the trail behind him, a plastic grocery-store bag in her hand which, when he looked at it, she tucked behind her back.

"Did you need something?" she asked.

He nearly laughed, nearly fell on his knees under the force of all the things he wanted. He opened his mouth but only a rattling gasp came out. Silence.

"Gabe?" Her voice was that soft pet, the delicious stroke against his body, and he wanted to pull her into his arms one last time. Banish the demons, the past, the specter of the future.

"Just wanted to make sure everything was going okay," he said. "We've been so busy I never get a chance to see you."

"I know. It's like I blink and three days have passed. But everything seems to be going really well."

"That's making me nervous."

She laughed and the tension in him balled tighter.

"Oh, I forgot to tell you, Tim Munoz has taken the job. He'll be here on the twenty-fourth, so I can stay or—"

"That's fine. Thank you."

He was too abrupt, too close to apologizing, to asking for another chance, another doomed chance.

"Good night," he said and walked away, into the dark.

"Good night, Gabe." Her voice chased him all the way back to the lodge, to his empty cold bed.

The world cracked, opened and then closed again, different now than it had been before Alice looked at the stick. Pregnant.

She tore open the plastic around the second test, downed a glass of water, peed, waited and got the same blue plus sign in the window.

The earth dazzled, sparkled; her small cottage was the epicenter of the universe. Of creation.

She pulled in air that tasted like sugar and salt. Her heart pumped blood through her body, through the small tadpole deep in her belly.

"A baby." She sighed, the words delicious on her tongue, the prospect all she would need to sustain her. For months. Years. Her life.

She put her hand to her mouth to stifle the laughing sobs. The giddy screams of joy and panic. Alice collapsed onto the toilet, slid sideways when she miscalculated and she landed on the floor. She lay back, flung her arms out and laughed at the ceiling.

A baby.

The world was filled with blessings and second chances.

Gabe.

She put her hands to her face, kicked her feet against the wall in a sudden thrilled spasm.

Gabe standing in front of her cabin, looking for the whole world, like a boy lost in a mall. She could give him a second chance, them a second chance. Another shot to make it work.

Tears burned down her face into her mouth, a champagne of hope and wish.

But soon the tiles grew cold against her back and what would be settled around her like a curtain, a screen showing old home movies of their life before the divorce.

She'd tell him she was pregnant and Gabe, honorable and longing for a family, would propose.

She didn't want that marriage. She didn't want him that way, tied to her by this fragile pregnancy. What she wanted them to have had to be real.

Gabe couldn't know. Not yet.

17

"I've requested a few more servers from the catering company in Albany," Gabe said to Alice and the rest of his staff in the kitchen the morning of the rehearsal dinner. Alice barely listened, still blissfully distracted by her pregnancy.

Gabe's confidence in this staff, including Cameron and her folks, was tangible. He treated everyone like a team member and they listened to him like the good boss he was. Affection, a great tidal wave of love for everyone in this room, washed over her, and she bit her lip to keep her eyes from welling with happy tears.

"These people are drinkers and we're going to need the extra hands just to get rid of the bottles and empty glasses," Gabe said. "We don't want it to look like a teamsters' picnic."

"We've added a few heartier appetizers," her father said. "Maybe we can keep the drinkers from getting too drunk too fast."

What a guy, she thought, looking at her dad. She wished she could tell him he was going to be a grandfather, but the past had taught her to keep the joy silent until it was a sure thing.

She looked at Gabe and felt paralyzed by the choice she had to make, the news she was keeping from him. Was it for his own good? Or hers?

"Excellent idea, Michael," Gabe said, and the meeting broke up, everyone heading to their last-minute duties. Alice watched Gabe head to his office and took a step to follow. To say what? To do what? She didn't know, she just knew she wanted to be close to him.

"Can I talk to you for a second?" Max asked, touching her elbow slightly.

"Sure," she said, eager for the distraction. "What's up?"

"Outside," Max said and opened the door for her to step into the beautiful June morning.

Surprised, she walked over to the small hill with the view of the lawn and gazebo, which were getting decked out in fine style.

"What's going on with you?" Max asked, cutting to the chase.

Alice nearly blanched. "What do you mean?"

"I mean, what's going on? You're—" He blew out a breath. "You're happy. Gabe's a wreck. I haven't seen either of you like this since—" He stopped suddenly and Alice could actually see the math in his head, the wheels turning. "Are you pregnant?"

For a moment she was able to pretend she was going to lie about this, that she had the capability to keep a straight face when fireworks were going off in her head. But then she smiled.

Max flung his hands in the air. "That explains it. Gabe's just worried about another miscarriage."

"Gabe doesn't know."

Max's mouth fell open slightly. "You haven't told him? You're pregnant after everything you two went through and you're not telling him?"

"Yet. I'm not telling him *yet*." She stepped closer and considering how right she believed she was, she had no problem standing up to her tough former brother-in-law. "If he and I are going to make it work, he needs to come back to me for me. Not because I'm pregnant and he's trying to do the right thing, or to get his shot at a family. It has to be about us, first and foremost."

Max stared at her a long time, and Alice kept his gaze. "Sounds reasonable. But he's got to know at some point. You can't walk away from him with his baby."

"What if I lose the baby, Max? What then?"

He shook his head, clearly understanding her dilemma. "So, what are you going to do?"

"I am going to..." She took a long breath and let it out. "I'm going to give him another chance to try to make it work without knowing about the baby. If he's still too scared, then I'm going to leave and talk to my doctor and then..." She took another long breath. She really hadn't thought this out very well. "If everything seems good, I'll contact him."

"When?"

"When I think it's right."

"You're going to do it all by yourself?"

"If he's too scared to try to make it work with me before I go, then—" she swallowed "—yes."

He shook his head. "Not acceptable."

"Excuse me?"

"First of all, you shouldn't do all of it alone. Bed rest and doctor's appointments and whatever else you're going to have to do to carry this baby the whole way and, second—" Max's eyes went soft for a moment "—it's Gabe's baby."

Her stomach melted into her feet. "I know, Max. But it would kill me to have him ask me to stay because of a baby. We did that before and it failed miserably. I need to know it's about me. Us. That we could make it together if I lost this baby."

Max didn't blink. He didn't move until finally he nodded, once. Definitively.

"You have two months and if Gabe doesn't hear from you, I'm sending him to you to tell him."

"Max—"

"That's the deal, Alice. He's my brother and if you won't look out for him, I will."

Alice nodded. It was fair. It was ugly and weird, but it was fair. And she truly hoped, in the end, it wouldn't come to that.

"Hey, hey." He pulled her into his arms, a big hard hug that made it difficult to breathe. "Congrats, Alice," he murmured against her hair. "I know how bad you want this. But remember, so does Gabe."

"I know," she whispered. It was the thought that plagued her.

The rehearsal dinner rolled around and Gabe had asked Alice to play hostess with him, so she kept her chef whites in the closet and pulled out the one dress she'd brought for the event. A black kimono-style dress with an embroidered cherry tree along the side. It skimmed over her body, form-fitting but not too tight. She endured, for the sake of fashion, a pair of modest high heels, that made her feet hurt just looking at them.

She kept her hair down, brushed to a blue-black shine and for once, not an unruly curl in sight.

At the last minute, she added the mascara she knew her mother would hound her over and a bit of red lip gloss.

All of which was worth the effort when she walked into the dining room, and Gabe, giving last-minute instructions to the two bartenders working the event, glanced at her then did a quick double take.

Patrick, looking dashing in a suit and tie, whistled. Max, still in his flannel shirt and fleece, looked at her and mouthed, "Tonight."

She scowled at him and joined Gabe at the bar.

"You look beautiful," he said.

"You're not too shabby yourself," she said, straightening the collar on his black shirt. Her hand lingered, touched the plane of his chest, felt the thump of his heart under her hand.

"You okay?" he asked, just barely touching her wrist.

"Yes." She lifted her hand to her forehead. "I am, but I—"

"Hold that thought, Al. We've got mother of the bride at three o'clock, looking mad."

Gabe stepped away to intercept Gloria, and Alice sagged briefly against the bar.

"Club soda, please," she said to the bartender and she avoided Max's pointed look.

The rehearsal dinner passed in a blur. The sea bass was well received, but perhaps not hearty enough to counter all the alcohol the party went through. Alice was called into duty to help various women with safety pins and tissues. She directed a drunk bridesmaid out back with the rest of the smokers and noticed the great-aunt of the bride was sitting alone at one of the dark tables while the speeches got started. She brought the woman a cup of tea just as the sound system screeched and Patrick was called into duty to fix it.

"That's not a good sound," Alice joked, setting the teacup in front of the older woman.

"If that's the only thing that goes wrong, sweetheart," she said, "you'll be laughing. So far this is the most beautiful event I've ever seen."

"Well, there's tomorrow. Things could still go plenty wrong."

She patted Alice's hands. "I'm ninety years old and I've seen a lot of weddings. You have to trust me. You and your husband have done a very nice job."

Alice was about to protest their marital state but she looked up to see Gabe in the shadows, his bright eyes on her, burning her through the darkness, and she couldn't say anything.

At three in the morning, Gabe shot up in bed, startled out of a fitful sleep by what sounded like a gang of fighting toddlers. He pulled on the dress pants he'd shucked just a few hours ago and slid into his work boots before racing out into the front yard to see what was killing what and making so much noise.

Alice, in sweatpants and a chef jacket, her hair a wild halo around her head, was already there.

"What the hell is that noise?" she asked, peering into the dark, flashlight in hand. "It's freaking me out."

"I don't know," Gabe murmured. He turned toward the tent they'd erected for the ceremony only to see the canvas sides roll as if they were being buffeted by gale-force winds. "But it's in my tent."

They took a few cautious steps in that direction before Max was suddenly with them, in boxer shorts, work boots and a T-shirt.

"You guys making all that noise?" He growled the words, rubbing at his whiskered face.

"It's racoons," Patrick said, stomping past them armed with two old hockey sticks, one of which he tossed to Gabe as if he were John Wayne and they were about to fight marauding invaders.

"Raccoons?" Gabe asked. "In my tent?"

They pulled open the front flap to a scene of heart-breaking destruction. Most of the chairs were on their sides, and the topiaries with the fancy bows that had taken hours to tie were toppled over and half eaten.

"Oh, no," Alice cried, and Gabe, furious and exhausted, caught sight of one of the giant mutant raccoons eating a bow and chased it, stick held high, out of the tent.

All along he'd expected something to go wrong. Some miscalculation or dropped detail. He hadn't counted on Mother Nature sending rabid minions to destroy the event he'd sunk way too much time and money into.

Max joined in, clapping and yelling and corralling the animals in a corner so Patrick could chase them out one of the flaps.

Alice screamed. Gabe whirled and found her cornered by one of the animals, using a chair to keep him away from the topiary she was trying to repair.

"There's a whole forest out there!" she cried. "Get. Scat. Shoo."

Gabe charged, wielding his hockey stick like a giant ax, and the raccoon abandoned his campaign, turned tail and ran down the center aisle and out the front of the tent.

In silence Gabe took in the destruction. Half the topiaries were toast. The ribbons were a mess. The chairs were filthy and he'd stepped in raccoon poop. They all had. Raccoon poop was everywhere.

"No." He moaned. "No. This is a disaster."

"We'll get it fixed up, Gabe." Alice said, patting his shoulder. "I'll go put on a pot of coffee and get some rags and hot water."

"I'll come with you," Max said. "We need some trash bags."

"No one will ever know, son," Patrick told him and started righting the folding chairs and picking up what was left of the flower decorations.

By ten a.m., moments before the bride walked down the aisle, no one would have believed that hours ago the scene had been chaos. Carnage. The stuff of wedding disaster.

Nope, Gabe thought with satisfaction and a deep exhaustion. *You'd never guess I was picking up raccoon crap in my underwear in the middle of the night.*

Grandmothers were escorted in to Pachelbel's Canon in D and Gabe stifled a yawn under his palm.

"Looks good," Alice said from behind him. He turned, relieved in some deep place to have her next to him. The way he had been all night as they worked side by side until dawn, fixing the tent.

"Well, your idea to spread out the topiaries and scrap the bows altogether certainly made it easier."

"I only suggested it so I wouldn't be on poop patrol," she said. Her hand on his arm burned through the sleeve of his black jacket and the white linen shirt beneath that to his skin, muscle and bone. "It looks beautiful, Gabe."

Just a touch and he was branded.

"Well, I couldn't have done it without you," he told her, making a point of not looking at her. He could do this. He could tell her the truth and say goodbye as long as he didn't have to say it to her face. "I owe you."

She didn't say anything and her silence forced him to glance at her. Tears trembled on her lashes, turning her dark eyes to obsidian.

"Alice?" he asked, startled by this sudden emotion. "What's—"

She rose on her toes and pressed a wet kiss to his cheek. "You don't owe me anything, but we have to talk."

He shook his head, knowing instinctively what she meant. "There's nothing to say, Alice. You know that. We've—"

"A conversation. That's what you owe me." Something fierce in her wet gaze made him nod his head.

"Okay," he agreed softly as the sweet swell of "Ode to Joy" started. The bride arrived at the tent and the audience gasped, coming to its feet.

∾

The music pumped and the lights twinkled. Couples danced, bridesmaids kicked off their shoes and Gabe quietly folded in the corner. He rubbed his eyes and wished he could put his head down on the table and sleep for a week.

"Hey, Gabe." A little voice at his elbow made him open his eyes. Helen. He smiled, glad that Alice had invited Daphne and her daughter, because the little girl had twirled nonstop for hours. The bride had noticed her initially and asked her to dance and Helen had leaped around like a jack-in-the-box come to life.

"Hi, sweetie," he said and pulled on her long ponytail. "You look like a princess. Have I told you that?"

"Like a thousand times, but I want to dance." She jumped up and down in her scuffed black patent shoes.

"Then we dance," he said. Luckily, the music changed and the singer crooned an old blues song about love coming at last.

He spun her dramatically and dipped her upside down and sang the words off-key so she'd giggle and hold on tight to the lapels of his jacket.

Finally she laid her head on his shoulder and he held her and swayed a little bit, his heart a puddle in his shoes.

"It's time to take her home," Daphne said at his elbow. "She's out like a light." Daphne looked tired but happy and still elegant in her red dress. She'd caught the eye of one of the ushers and Daphne had been out on the dance floor almost as much as her daughter. "Here," she said, reaching for her.

"I got it," Gabe whispered. "I'll take her to your car. No sense in waking her if we don't have to."

Daphne nodded and led Gabe out the front doors, grabbing her purse and shoes from under one of the tables.

"It was a beautiful night, Gabe," she said, walking to her

sedan parked in the employee area behind the kitchen. "You did a great job."

"Well, it was a team effort." He deferred the glory, gladly. "Alice really deserves the kudos."

"She told me about the raccoons," Daphne laughed and shook her head as she unlocked her car. "Unbelievable."

Gabe eased the little girl into her booster seat in the backseat and it was a testament to her exhaustion that she barely stirred while Daphne clipped her in.

"How is it going with Alice?" Daphne asked, standing up. "If you don't mind me asking."

"It's not. Going, I mean. We never should have tried in the first place."

"I'm sorry to hear that."

He tucked his hands in his pockets and nodded. *Not as sorry as me*, he thought.

She reached up and kissed his cheek. The gesture didn't even register a spark or flutter. Nothing. Daphne stepped away and he could tell in her eyes that she didn't feel anything, either.

"You need to listen when the universe tries to tell you something, I guess," she said. "You and I were meant to be friends."

"Good friends," he agreed and watched as she climbed into her car and drove away.

He wondered what the universe meant for him and Alice. What were they supposed to be?

"Gabe?"

He turned, and Alice, stepping over the small hill behind him, arrived.

He felt solemn. Sad even. His arms were heavy and empty and his chest, where the little girl had slept, cold.

"It seemed like Helen had a good time," she said and they watched the taillights disappear down the road.

He nodded, words clogged in his throat, stuck behind emotions and a sickening lack of courage.

"She's the exact age our daughter would have been," she said and his eyes slid closed as grief lanced him.

I know.

"I won't ask you to talk about the children we didn't have," she said. "But I need you to know that I love you, Gabe," Alice whispered, her sweet voice tying ribbons around him, wrapping him up. "I am in love with you. I always have been and I probably always will be."

He swallowed and the cowardice bobbed but remained stuck. He kept his eyes on the horizon, like a seasick sailor longing for solid ground.

"I want to stay here." Her voice grew rougher, and he knew that his silence was making her angry, so he finally turned to her. She blazed and burned, casting a light that could keep him warm his entire life if he only would reach for it.

"I want to keep working on this dream." She tilted her head. "On our dream." She searched his face. "Don't you have anything to say?" Tears gathered in her eyes and he felt the same burn in his. This constant echo of emotion between them. Whatever she felt, he did, too. It was exhausting. Destructive.

"What happens when things go wrong, Alice?" he asked, his voice scorched and burned by the heat of his barely contained emotions. "What do we do when the fights start?"

"We're older now, Gabe. We're different. We'll handle it better. Look at today. We were a team today."

He nodded. "Today. But two months ago I tried to fire

you because you drank too much. Are you trying to tell me that we've changed that much in two months."

"Yes. I have. I have changed that much." She waited for his answer, no doubt longing for him to finally realize that he'd changed, too. That being back together, that seeing the success of this place had cleared the old cobwebs from his head and he was ready to start a different life as a different person.

But he wasn't. He was the same. And slowly, as he watched her face, he saw her recognize that. His heart shattered when he watched the love in her eyes grow cold, turn to disbelief. Anger.

"I'm sorry," he whispered. "I can't take the risk."

"The risk that we won't have children?" she asked. "That we won't be able to adopt if it comes to that?"

He shook his head, opened his mouth. There was nothing but silence. He didn't know how to say what he felt.

"You can't take the risk of loving me and having me leave," she said. "Like your mom."

A hot tear seared down the side of his face.

"Like my mom, like those babies—" his voice cracked. "Our babies. I can't." He shook his head. "I wanted them, too, Alice." He finally told her, an avalanche of words accompanied by more hot tears scalding his skin. "I named them when you said we should wait and see what they were like." He closed his eyes, doing his best to shove these memories of Daniel and Chloe—his children—away. He rubbed his hands in his eyes, brushing away the tears. He mentally shook himself, took a deep breath and looked Alice in the face.

"Let's stop pretending that everything is great, Alice. It's not. As a couple you and I are always on the edge of disaster and I can't live like that."

She laughed. "Everyone is on the edge of disaster. Everyone. Love puts you there. You think having a relationship with a woman you don't love is going to keep you safe?"

"Not being in a relationship with you will keep me safe," he told her and watched his words hit home. She practically shrank and he wished he could take them back to spare her this truth, but she wouldn't leave well enough alone.

She stepped backward, nearly tripped, but found her ground.

"You're a fool, Gabe," she said, turned and left.

Fool or not, he needed security, a security they'd never found together. Inside the dining room, the party raged on, his inn a success, his future, for the moment, set.

And he had never in his whole life felt so hollow.

Alice curled up on her bed, her hands cupped over her stomach as if that could protect her unborn child from all those things that could cause pain. Grief. Bone-deep loss.

She wished, stupidly, despite the rejection that she could do the same for Gabe. But it was impossible.

Grabbing the cell phone off the bedside table, she wiped her eyes and called her parents. They'd left hours ago but she knew her dad would only be dozing in front of the TV.

"Dad," she said when he answered, sleepy and gruff.

"Hi, sweetie," he said. "Everything okay?"

She bit her lips but the tears came anyway. "No, Dad," she whispered. "I need a favor."

18

Gabe came downstairs, braced for Alice. For seeing her, for her cold shoulder and red-rimmed eyes. So when he stepped into the kitchen at dawn, the last thing he expected to see was Michael. Sharpening knives.

"Good morning, Gabe," he said over the vicious *snick-snick* of his chef's blade running along the sharpener.

"Michael." He nodded and took the long way around the giant man with knives toward the coffeepot. "Where's Alice?"

"Albany, by now, I'd imagine."

Hot coffee sloshed over his hand. "She left." It was more statement than question. And Michael nodded, eyeing the edge of his knife, like a pirate about to commit murder.

"Did she say why?"

"No." Michael turned to him. "But she asked me to fill in for the next two weeks and she was crying. Know anything about that?"

Gabe put down the coffeepot with shaking hands. It was over. Done. He didn't have to worry about seeing her again every day, about the constant temptation of knowing she was within reach.

Turning from Michael and the threat of decapitation, Gabe put his hand to his forehead, a helpless moment to get himself under control.

"Thank you, Michael,' he managed to whisper, throwing a quick smile over his shoulder, "for filling in."

Michael slapped his knife down on the butcher's block. "Jesus, you kids are killing each other."

"It's what we've always done best," Gabe said and went into his office in an effort to lose himself in work.

Patrick didn't even bother going to the gazebo when a driver finally delivered the letter. Patrick ripped it open in the driveway, reading it before the driver was even back in the car.

He'd expected a response right away. Truth be told he'd expected Iris right away. But as every day went by with no Iris and no letter, that hope turned to cement and filled his body.

Patrick,

Thank you. Thank you so much. I will be there, but I need time. It's not what you think. But I need a few months. I will be there. Trust me. For once, I will be there.

Patrick scowled, heartbroken and disappointed and angry that he was actually disappointed. He crumpled the letter, unable to save this one. He'd believed her earnest and genuine desire to come here, to make things right. But he should have remembered the way his wife could turn on a dime.

Now, he didn't know what to believe.

Gabe stared blindly at the *Bon Appetit* spread on his desk. A rave review, pictures that made his inn look like something outside of himself, something he'd never seen before. The only reason he recognized it was because he and Alice were standing at the front doors in the first picture.

"Congratulations," Michael said, his backpack over his shoulder, ready to go. "It's a great article. You should get lots of business from it."

Gabe couldn't find the will to respond.

"Tim is going to be an excellent addition here," Michael continued, but he might as well have been speaking French. "He's got a lot of great ideas."

"How is she?" he asked off the conversation topic, but she was the only thing he thought about these days. "Alice. How is she?"

"I won't be your go-between, Gabe. My daughter is an adult. If you want to find out how she is, be an adult and call her." Michael waited for him to say something, but there was nothing to say. Finally he shook his head in disgust and left.

God, Gabe sighed and kicked away from his desk, the contact of his foot against the metal felt good. Violent.

He'd thought things would get better after Alice left. He would find some clarity. Get back to being himself.

But nothing got better.

The final payment from the Crimpsons, along with a lovely thank-you note and photograph, arrived, followed by two phone calls from women who had been at the wedding and wanted to talk about having an event at the inn.

He didn't know what to promise them. Alice, who had made all the magic possible for the Crimpsons, was gone and the magic was absolutely absent without her.

But he talked to the new clients and made empty promises that sounded good but echoed falsely in his mouth.

Alice was right, he realized as he told these women what they wanted to hear. It's win-win until it all goes to crap.

And it had definitely gone to crap.

"Gabe." Max stood at the door, his forehead creased with concern. "What's wrong? Did you hear from Alice?"

If only. If only he'd heard from her and this ache might leave, this boulder on his chest might be rolled away.

"Did she say something? Are you going to Albany?"

"No!" Gabe yelled, the boulder making him scream. Making him crazy. "She has not called. She's gone. Let's all get on with our lives, okay?"

Max blinked at him, no doubt stunned by this sudden vehemence. "You're doing a hell of job with that," Max said. "Really moving on without her."

"Shut up," Gabe yelled. He stood up from his desk, the chair spinning out behind him to smash into the wall. Gabe shoved his brother out of the door frame, and then gripped the door as hard as he could and hurled it shut. The walls shook from the force.

Blood and anger pounded in his brain. And slamming

doors wasn't enough. He kicked the empty cardboard boxes in the corner.

Still not enough.

He picked up the jar of pens on his desk and smashed it against the wall. He swept the desk lamp off, his, the shattering of glass a sweet stroke to his rage.

What is wrong with me?

Why do they always leave?

Why can't I keep the people I love close to me?

He was blind, reckless. Objects found their way against walls, under his feet. Destroyed by his hands. He didn't feel cuts or blood or physical pain.

He felt only grief—a bottomless pit of grief that could no longer be ignored.

∾

Patrick jumped back from the office door when it sounded as if a chair had been hurled into it.

He and Max had been standing there for the better part of ten minutes and whatever was going on behind that door was not slowing down.

"He's really going for it," Patrick said. "There can't be much left of that chair."

Max nodded and took a sip from his coffee cup that was filled with scotch. Patrick had one, too. They were preparing themselves for what would happen when Gabe finally stopped destroying his office and opened the door.

"What's going on here?" Tim, the new chef—a nice guy having a really bad first day—asked. He set down the box of kitchen stuff he'd brought in from his car and flinched as

Gabe howled from behind the door, sounding like a man who had lost everything.

Which, Patrick supposed, he had.

"Is everything okay?" Tim's eyes were worried behind his dark oblong glasses. He pulled his shirt away from his belly and practically twitched from the tension in his kitchen.

"My son's just working a few things out," Patrick answered over the strains of smashing glass.

"Here," Max said, grabbing a coffee cup from the counter and filling it from the bottle of scotch at his feet. "Welcome to the Riverview Inn."

Tim took the scotch and tossed it back. "I hope it gets better than this," he muttered and they all laughed.

Finally, abruptly the office door opened and his son, shattered and bleeding from a cut on his hand and another one above his eyes, stood there.

Crying.

"Come on, son," Patrick said, feeling the bite of tears in his own eyes. "Let's get you cleaned up."

"It hurts, Dad," he whispered.

"What does, son?"

"Everything."

∼

Gabe felt as if he'd been hit by a truck. As if he had no bones in his body. After his dad bandaged him up, Max herded all of them to the couches in the dining room. He tried to get all of them to have a drink—his kind of therapy. But Gabe didn't have the taste for it.

Tim, his new chef, sat next to him looking a little shell-shocked.

"It's not usually like this," Gabe said, patting Tim's bent knee.

"Right. Usually there are raccoons running wild," Max said into his own coffee mug.

"Raccoons?" Tim asked.

"He's kidding." Gabe assured him, then decided the truth from here on out would feel better. "Sort of."

Tim took another swig from his mug. And Gabe concentrated on breathing. On his sudden longing for canned tomato soup, Oreos and Alice.

I want Alice.

I just want her back.

"Consider this an initiation, Tim," Patrick said. "The Men's Club of Broken Hearts, Eastern New York Division."

The pain, the guilt and confusion in Gabe's chest coalesced and spun faster, growing bigger. He shifted in his seat, trying to make room for what was happening to him.

Tim smiled, the dimple showing up in his cheek. "I've had a broken heart once or twice."

"The price of admission," Patrick said and Tim laughed.

Max simply watched Gabe from the other couch as if he saw right through him.

"Welcome to the rest of your life," Max said and toasted Gabe.

And just like that Gabe was on his feet. The hurricane in his chest taking over his body. He didn't want this for the rest of his life.

He wanted Alice. Good or bad. Because sadly, there was no good without her anymore.

Maybe she was right. Maybe they were different. Older. Wiser. He just had to trust that, trust what they had.

"I gotta go," he said.

"Where?" Patrick asked.

"Albany."

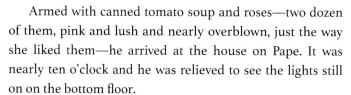

Armed with canned tomato soup and roses—two dozen of them, pink and lush and nearly overblown, just the way she liked them—he arrived at the house on Pape. It was nearly ten o'clock and he was relieved to see the lights still on on the bottom floor.

The truck was barely parked before he'd leaped out, roses and cans of soup in hand. It had been a little over two weeks, surely her feelings for him couldn't have changed. She'd be mad, sure, angry that it took him so long to get his head out of the sand, but in the end, after he groveled, after he told her all the dreams he'd had for those children who had died, all the dreams he had for the children they now would have, by whatever means, she'd be happy.

He'd talk about his mother, about how he still felt like that kid sitting at the kitchen table waiting for his mom to come home.

He'd tell her that nothing was worth having if she wasn't there to share it. He'd tell her anything she wanted to hear.

It would work, eventually.

It had to—his life depended on it.

But his palms were still sweating and his heart still thudded and he hoped he wouldn't be forced to use the key under the frog.

Surprisingly, the door opened under his light knock and he poked his head into the hallway.

"Charlie?" Alice's voice came from the living room in the back of the house. "Come on in! I'm starved."

He stepped in and walked down the hallway hoping her reaction would be a good one. Surprise, sure. Joy, if he was lucky.

Please let me be lucky.

"I hope you remembered the vinegar because I hate—"

"Ketchup on your fries," he finished her sentence as he stepped into the living room.

She was camped out on the couch, Felix in her lap. The two of them surrounded by magazines, water glasses and McDonald's French fry containers.

And the look on her face was not joy. It was horror, quickly being replaced by rage.

Horror and rage. Not at all what he'd expected.

Felix leaped off her lap to curl around his ankles.

"What are you doing here?" she asked, plucking at the collar of the ratty David Hasselhoff T-shirt she wore when she felt sick and in need of comfort.

"Seeing the patient?" he tried to joke. "The Hoff and French fries—you must not be feeling very good."

"I feel fine. Did Max send you here?"

He laughed. "In a way."

Alice huffed through her nose like a bull about to stampede and hiked herself up farther on the pillows. "Great, and now you're here to do the right thing."

"Well, I think so. I mean. It's—Why are you angry?"

Felix, no doubt sensing the volatile atmosphere, took off.

"Why? Because your being here because you have to be isn't the way I want you. I want you here of your own free will, because you want me. Because life without me sucks."

"It does." He shook his head. "I'm missing something here."

"Yeah, right. Your shot at a family. I get it." She put her feet on the floor and began to stand and Gabe pushed her back against the couch.

"I'm here because I don't want to be like Max. I'm here because my life is terrible without you. Food tastes like dirt. Success feels hollow and the Riverview Inn is empty without you in the kitchen. And yes, I want a family. I thought that was the point."

Alice started to cry, staring at the ceiling as tears rolled down her face. She wiped at them with her T-shirt.

"Alice." He set down the roses and got down on his knees in front of her to touch her, offer whatever comfort he could. She pushed him away. Smacked his hands until he finally sat back. "What am I missing?"

"What happens if something goes wrong, remember? That's what you said. So what if I lose this baby and you're here and you hate—"

"This baby?" he asked, slowly because his brain was imploding.

Finally she looked at him, stared right into his lost soul. "You don't know."

"What don't I know? Exactly."

"You're here on your own? You're here—"

"Because I love you. I'm in love with you and always will be. Now tell me what's going on." He gripped her hands, hard, an anchor in this sudden void he'd been dropped in.

"I'm pregnant."

"You're—" He fell back on his butt. "What?"

"Seven weeks," she said, looking like a princess, regal and above touch. "I'm seven weeks' pregnant."

He was sweating. Buckets. It rolled down his back, flooded his eyes. "Are you...okay?"

"Dr. Johnson says yes. He says I need to rest whenever

possible—" She gestured to the couch behind her.

He swallowed. "Are you...happy? I mean to be pregnant again."

"Yes," she said fiercely.

"Are you happy to be pregnant with my baby?" he asked, poised on the edge of a knife.

"I'm not sure yet," she whispered. "You're kind of a jerk."

He bit back the sudden bark of laughter. She needed some groveling and rightfully so.

"Al. You are my life. Baby or no. Family or no. Nothing is good without you. My life is empty. My inn is empty. My dream, our dream, is a shell without you. And I will spend the rest of my life trying to fill your life as you have mine."

"And—"

He laughed, but the sound rattled with tears and emotion. "And I will spend the rest of my life apologizing for being a jerk. Now, before I die of a heart attack, are you happy to be pregnant with my baby?"

She lurched forward, tears magnifying her stunning black eyes, and grabbed his face. "I am so happy to be pregnant with your baby. No matter what happens."

He gripped her hands on his face, holding tight to her, looking right back at her, seeing all their flaws collectively and separately and still wanting to make it work. "You weren't going to tell me?"

"Not until I knew I was out of the woods." She stroked his face carefully, with just her thumb. Tentative. "I didn't want you to be obligated to me. I wanted you to love *me*."

"I do. Oh, you have no idea how much I love you." He pulled her into his arms, across his lap, held her as close as he could, tried to soak her into his skin, through his bones and muscle so they would never be apart.

He pressed his lips to her head, tears fell into her hair

and he couldn't stop laughing.

"So, you're happy?" she asked against his neck, her arms locked around his back. "I mean, you're not mad?"

"Well, you have to explain why Max knew before me but —" he shook his head, stroking her hair away from her beloved face "—no. I'm not mad. I'm nervous. I'm worried. I'm so happy I think I might throw up."

"I've been doing enough of that for both of us," she said, making a face. "I guess we have a lot to talk about, huh?"

"I want you back at the inn," he said. "You won't have to lift a finger. I'll be your personal French fry slave."

"Hmm, sounds good," she said and kissed him.

Her lush familiar beautiful lips pressed to his, her body, changing right under his hands, the future spreading out before them with endless possibility.

They still had things to deal with—but they could handle it. No matter what came their way.

"Sounds like heaven," he said.

WANT MORE of THE RIVERVIEW INN? Learn Max's secrets in SECRETS OF THE RIVERVIEW INN. Keep reading for an exclusive excerpt....

CHAPTER ONE

Max Mitchell slid the two-by-four over the sawhorses and brushed the snow off his hand tools, but more fat flakes fell to replace what he'd moved.

It was only nine in the morning, and the forecast had called for squalls all day.

Winter. Nothing good about it.

Of course, spending every minute of the season outside was a surefire way to cultivate his dislike of the cold. But lately, walls no matter how far away—and ceilings—no matter how high—felt too close. Like coffins.

The thick brown gloves didn't keep out the chill so he clapped his hands together, scaring blackbirds from the tree line a few feet behind him.

Even the skeleton structure he'd spent the past few months constructing seemed to shiver and quake in the cold December morning.

He eyed his building and for about the hundredth time he wondered what it was going to be.

It wasn't one of the cottages that he'd spent last spring and summer building for his brother's Riverview Inn.

Too small for that. Too plain for his brother, Gabe, the owner of the luxury lodge in the wilderness of the Catskills.

Max told everyone it was going to be an equipment shed, because they needed one. But it was so far away from the buildings that needed maintaining and the lawns that needed mowing, he knew it would be a pain in the butt hauling equipment back and forth.

Still, he called it a shed because he didn't know what else to call it.

Besides, the construction kept his hands busy, his head empty. And busy hands and an empty head stymied the worst of the memories.

The skin on the back of his neck grew knees and crawled for his hairline and he whirled, one hand at his hip as if his gun would be where it had been for ten years. But of course his hip was empty and, behind him, watching him silently beneath a snow-covered Douglas fir, was a little girl.

"Hi," he said.

She waved.

"You by yourself?" He scanned the treeline for a parent.

She nodded.

Talkative little thing.

"Where'd you come from?" Max asked.

The girl jerked her thumb toward the inn that was back down the trail about thirty feet through the forest.

"Are you a guest?" he asked, although it was Monday and most guests checked in on Sunday. "At the inn?"

She shrugged.

"You...ah...lost?" Max asked.

She shook her head.

"Can you talk?"

She nodded.

"Are you gonna?"

She shook her head and smiled.

His heart, despite the hours in the cold, warmed his chest.

"Do you think maybe someone is worried about you?"

At that the girl stopped smiling and glanced behind her at the buildings barely visible through the pines.

"Should we head back?" he asked, stepping away from his project in forgetting. At his movement she darted left, away from the trail, under the heavy branches of trees and he stopped.

She was a deer ready to run. And since beyond him there was a whole lot of nothing, he figured he'd best keep her here until someone came looking for her.

"All right," he said. "We don't have to go anywhere."

Amongst the trees, her pink coat partially hidden in shadows, he saw her pink-gloved finger point at the building behind him.

"It's a house," he said.

She laughed, the bright tinkle filling his silent clearing.

"You think it's too small?" he asked, and her head nodded vigorously.

"Well, it's for a very small family—" he eased slightly closer to her where she hid "—of racoons."

Something crunched under his foot and she zipped deeper into the shadows and now he couldn't see her face. He stopped.

Two years off the force and he'd lost his touch.

"Want to play a game?" he asked, and when she didn't answer and didn't run he took it for a yes. "I'm going to guess how old you are and if I guess right, we go inside, because it's too cold." He shivered dramatically.

Again, no sound, no movement.

"All right." He closed his eyes and rubbed his temples. "It's coming to me. I can see a number and you are...forty-two."

She laughed. But when he took a step, the laughter stopped, as if it had been cut off by a knife. He stilled. "What am I—too low? Are you older?"

Her gloved hand reached out between tree limbs and her thumb pointed down. "You're younger?" He pretended to be amazed. "Okay, let me try...eight?"

No laughter and no hand.

For one delightful summer of his misspent youth, Max had been an age and weight guesser on Coney Island. He had a ridiculous intuition for such things and that summer it had gotten him laid more times than he could count.

Ah. Misspent youth.

"Am I right?" he asked.

She stepped out from underneath the tree, her face still, her eyes wary.

"Are you scared? Of going back?"

She shook her head and looked at the end of her bright

orange and pink scarf, playing with the tassels.

"You just don't want to?" he asked.

The little girl's eyes lifted to his and he saw a misery there that he totally understood. She didn't like what was back there.

"Tough one," he muttered.

"Josie!" The cry split through the quiet forest. "Josie! Where are you?" It was a woman's voice and she panicked. Scared.

"You Josie?" he asked the little girl, and her guilty expression was enough.

"She's here!" he yelled. "Stay on the trail and—"

A woman, petite and fair, erupted from the trees and nearly tripped into the clearing. Her wild eyes searched the area until they landed on Josie, small and pink and looking like she wished she could vanish.

"Oh my God!" the woman cried, hurtling herself through snow to practically slide on her knees in front of Josie. "Oh, Josie. I was so worried." She checked the little girl, cupped her cheeks in her own bare hands. The woman didn't even have a coat on.

"What did I say about wandering off?" the woman asked, snow gathering in her red hair. "What did I say? You can't do that, Josie. You can't scare me that way." Finally the woman hauled Josie into her arms but stayed on her knees, her blue jeans no doubt getting soaked through.

No coat. No gloves and now she was going to be wet.

He cleared his throat. "She's been with—"

Before he could even finish, the woman was on her feet, Josie sequestered behind her. The woman was braced for battle, a bear protecting her cub and Max had serious respect for that particular facet of motherhood and had no desire to screw with it.

He took a careful step away from the two females and lifted his eyes to look into the woman's in an effort to calm her down. He opened his mouth to tell her that he meant no harm, but the words died a quiet death in his throat.

There was a buzz in the air and under his jacket all the hair on his arms stood up.

I know you, he thought, looking into her radiant blue eyes. *I know all about you.* Her stiff shoulders and trembling lips told the tale more vividly than anything she might say. This woman was terrified of more than just losing her daughter momentarily. This was a woman—a beautiful woman—grappling with big fears.

And the big fears seemed to be winning.

Her eyes narrowed and he looked away, suddenly worried that she might see him as clearly as he saw her. Though he didn't know what she would detect in him—cobwebs and dark corners, probably.

"Who are you?" she asked.

"Max Mitchell," he answered calmly, despite the fact that his heart was pumping a mile a minute.

He needed this woman to get out of here. Take her silent daughter and leave.

"Your brother is Gabe? The owner?" He nodded and she relaxed, barely. "He said you were in charge of operations."

"I mow the lawn." He shrugged. "Shovel snow." Not quite the truth, but the fact that just about everything would grind to a halt these days if he wasn't here didn't seem like the kind of thing to discuss at this moment.

"You better head back. You—" He pointed at the wet patches on her jeans and the snow scattered across her bright blue sweater. Her tight, bright blue sweater. A mama bear in provocative clothes, Lord save him. "You are gonna get cold."

And my clearing is getting crowded.

The woman and girl were a pretty picture, surrounded by white snow and green trees. They were bright spots, almost electric seeming. He found it difficult to look away.

"I'm Delia," she said, her accent flavored by the south. Texas, maybe.

A redhead from Texas. Trouble if ever there was. And a woman from Texas without a winter coat or gloves, in a Catskill winter, had to be a guest.

The girl tugged on her mother's hand and Delia wrapped an arm around her.

"And this is my daughter, Josie."

Josie waved a finger at Max and he smiled.

"We're acquainted."

Delia didn't like that. Not one bit. Her lips went tight, and her pale skin, no doubt cold, went red. "We'll head on back. Don't bother yourself showing us the way."

He nodded, knowing when he'd been told to stay put.

They turned toward the trail and Max forced himself not to watch them as they walked away.

"What did I say about talking to strangers?" Delia asked.

"I didn't say a word, Mama," Josie said, her voice a quiet peep with enough sass to indicate she knew what she was doing.

Max couldn't help it, laughter gushed out of his throat, unstoppable.

Trouble, the two of them.

One-Click
The Secrets of the Riverview Inn
Home To Riverview Inn.
Christmas at the Riverview Inn
Second Chance at the Riverview Inn

Manufactured by Amazon.ca
Acheson, AB

15939652R00140